The Masters Review
ten stories

The Masters Review

The Masters Review Volume X
Stories Selected by Diane Cook
Edited by Cole Meyer, Melissa Hinshaw, and Brandon Williams

Front cover design by Chelsea Wales
Interior design by Kim Winternheimer

First printing.

ISBN: 978-1-7363695-4-8

© 2022 *The Masters Review*. Published annually by *The Masters Review*. All rights reserved. No part of this publication may be reproduced or reprinted without prior written permission of *The Masters Review*. To contact an author regarding rights and reprint permissions please contact *The Masters Review*. www.mastersreview.com

Printed in the USA

To receive new fiction, contest deadlines,
and other curated content right to your inbox,
send an email to newsletter@mastersreview.com

The Masters Review
ten stories

Volume X

John Darcy • Greg Schutz
• Monica Macansantos • Eliana Ramage •
Jennifer Dupree • Travis Eisenbise
• Eliza Robertson • Elissa C. Huang •
Emma Sloley • Chelsy Diaz Amaya • Robert Glick
• Tanya Bellehumeur-Allatt • Francis Walsh •
Anna Reeser • Megan Callahan
• Hilary Dean

Stories Selected by
Diane Cook

Contents

Editor's Note • ix
Introduction • xi

Do Not Duplicate • 1
A String of Lapis Beads • 15
A Long and Circuitous Path • 33
All That Is or Ever Was or Will Be • 39
Eight Years in the Making • 59
Comfort Animals • 63
Something to Do With Time • 83
Persimmon • 87
Never Stop Learning, and Other Things
I Learned Along the Way • 97
The Bird Rattle • 101
On Writing Into What We Don't Know • 117
Atlas, Bayonet, (War) Correspondence:
An Abecedarian • 121
Sugar • 139
A Person Who Writes • 153
Limbs • 157
Resurrection • 165

Editor's Note

Just over ten years ago, in an effort to fill the void that was left by the shuttering of the *Best New American Voices* anthology, *The Masters Review* opened its first call for submissions. That first volume, with finalists selected by Lauren Groff, paved the way for all that came after: nearly 300 stories and essays published online in our New Voices series, many of them debut writers, wonderful prizes given to our contest-winning writers, a chapbook (with another on the way) and now, 100 stories and essays published in our favorite project: *The Masters Review* Anthology.

There was never a doubt that Anthology X would be our biggest (dare I say Best?) anthology to date. Inside, you'll find our winning writers alongside essays from several of our former contributors, with advice for writers who were at one point in the very same shoes that our contributors to Anthology X are now. Selected by the fantastic Diane Cook, these ten new authors demonstrate the exquisite and wonderful magic of prose. (But I'll let her introduce you to their work.)

Thank you, from the bottom of our hearts, for your unending support over these terrific ten years.

—*Cole Meyer*
Editor-in-Chief

Introduction

In graduate school, I was a slush reader for a literary journal. I thought this type of thing could be my calling—discovering buried gems, dusting them off and showing everyone their worth. I was given a packet of stories to read and then all the readers met to choose which stories—if any—to pass to the editor. During my first meeting, I was surprised to hear that a story I had disliked wasn't just loved by everyone else, but loved SO MUCH that the question wasn't about whether we would accept it for publication, but that we might be too late because certainly it had been snapped up by another journal by now. I listened and tried to learn something, but honestly I was floored. In some part of my brain I understood it was an accomplished story, but I didn't understand what exactly that accomplishment was. A little later, a story that I loved came up for discussion. And I was floored again to find out not a single other person agreed. And perhaps it's just my own insecurity but I'm fairly certain they not only didn't agree, they kind of felt bad for me that I had liked this story and tried to advocate. I didn't walk away worried I was wrong. I walked away realizing that my time would be better spent writing the kind of work I liked, and not trying to figure out what everyone else in the room would be into.

That lingering memory has meant I approach judging contests with some hesitancy. Who am I to say what is the best? And what if no one sees what I see? Of course, we all realize at some point that nothing is universally good. Some people love things and some other people hate those same things, and even the most classic writing can be ravaged and torn apart by a reader who wishes to do so. Which can make contests such a minefield for writers, especially emerging ones.

When asked to judge for *The Masters Review*'s annual anthology, I was excited that they weren't asking me to pick a winner and runners-up. Instead, I would get to read and admire thirty excellent stories and then choose ten that could be combined to create something new. This wasn't just about finding the best stories, but the best collection of stories. To find stories that stood on their own, but stood out even more in the right company.

It led to interesting conversations with myself about what writing I find good and why. What I want a story to do to me. And the story after it, too. How formerly standalone pieces could now relate to one another, become something more by being in conversation. This was a much more satisfying task than ranking stories. I thought it also might be more satisfying to the writers themselves to become a part of something new and not just become a number.

As I read through the thirty (excellent!) stories, I noticed some leaving me with this *feeling*. I couldn't figure it out at first. I couldn't find words to describe it. It wasn't until I'd read all thirty that I realized that the stories I was still thinking about were the stories that had transported me. But that is a word that gets thrown around discussions of fiction, so what did I mean exactly? I mean that after reading them I felt like I had *traveled*. Not necessarily to a different or unfamiliar place, though some stories did that with setting. I mean that at some point between the first sentence and the last, I had been *moved*. Something in me changed because of what I'd witnessed. The reading had left me feeling altered. And I don't just mean mentally or emotionally or intellectually, but physically. Often after reading one of these ten stories, I felt like

I had spent energy, moved around, gotten lost and found inside the story. I felt the brain fatigue that sometimes accompanies real learning. Or the body exhaustion of trying to squeeze every last bit from an experience. Like I said, sometimes it was the setting that initiated this response. Other times it was the inner turmoil of a character. Sometimes the structure did it to me. Moved me around. *Transported me.* I realized I wanted to collect the stories that took me somewhere new, showed me the sights, and tired me out. Between the pages of a book I felt like I saw it all, and then I got to go home again.

Is anthology making my next calling? Probably not. But I love the work presented here and I feel grateful to each piece for shifting something inside me. These stories are their own worlds, with their own rituals, secrets, norms, sights, and even their own particular building codes. The writers are their own story's local expert. Let them show you around.

—Diane Cook
Guest Judge

Do Not Duplicate

John Darcy

When the guys finished the install last week, Bobby got all red in the jowls because I told him he's supposed to call it an accessibility ramp, not a wheelchair ramp. Bobby said, "Christ. You can't say anything anymore."

"But you just said it," I said. He's got hands the size of stocking caps that I can't help but be aware of in times like these.

"When are you gone for the thing?"

"Tomorrow and Friday," I said.

He told me not to get it in my head that he'll let me off early today. I said he'll have to kick me out tonight.

"Seems like just about the dumbest idea," he said, "that they're having it there."

I'd had the same thought, but that's how sober my brother is. "Bobby," I said. "My brother is so sober he can have his engagement party at a whiskey bar."

Bobby looked at me like I was speaking in tongues. "Not one minute early," he said.

* * *

Not that the competition is stiff—foodrunner at FoxHead Brewery, a questionable promotion to bartender, and before all that, three years as the worst radioman in the US Army—but Bobby's Key Shop is the best job I've ever had.

The sign out front says MORE KEYS THAN STARS IN THE SKY. Big peeling bubble letters on a stripped brick marquee, a defunct drive-in feel. Right above it is another sign: BOBBY'S KEY SHOP. Not an inch of wear or tear on that one. Bobby cleans it like a tabernacle, bathes it often with the fancy pressure washer he bought used from a supplier down in Illinois.

For ten dollars passed under the front counter, Bobby will say, "I don't see a thing," meaning the DO NOT DUPLICATE warning slapped on the collar of a key. Then he'll proceed in a receiptless transaction with any living soul.

He does it because this isn't the kind of place that installs those brainy, new home security systems. We're outdated, relics of relics, like ice farmers or pinsetters. We can't let you back into your car and we aren't locksmiths. We only sell keys here, and of course sometimes their counterparts.

I'm no big fan of Bobby's business model, but according to him it's the only way to keep the store afloat. "Motherfucker," he says with that toothless smile, "if I didn't do it, you wouldn't be here." He's basically one of those counterculture-boomers-in-reverse types, a late-life convert to the church of Ayn Rand. Still, we go back and forth over it, spar about the ethics. We trade blistering, usually personal, body blows. Bobby will throw out a jab, telling me I should quit if I really hate his practices. I counter with classic questions surrounding who he might have helped, and who he might have hurt. Which in my book is the only thing that matters, really, in the end, when it all comes down to it.

This is the angle I take today. That while yeah okay sure, most people want to clone their apartment key and nothing more, harmless. But what if there were one, one lone abuser or stalker or all-around creep trying to copy a pocketed key for his personal file, what then?

Bobby says, "So what are you saying, Teddy? That I might be a scumbag because I might have made a key for a person who might have done something bad?" He's got a soothing scar that snakes from the reddest nose I've ever seen to the smallest chin in the county. It's my great American pastime when I get him going on how he missed Woodstock by a "cunt hair." He thinks it makes for a more interesting story than if he actually would have gone. And who can blame him? I'm always in favor of watching the world whistle by.

"That's exactly right, boss." He thinks he has me. Those old-man eyebrows cannot tell a lie.

"You're a piece of work," Bobby says. "You're really something. You're the reason nobody wants to have kids anymore. What are we doing for lunch today?"

* * *

We lock up and jump over to the stoner sandwich joint on Gilman Street, a place Bobby hates to love. According to him it draws the wrong kind of characters into the outskirts of his store, but I can see the way he loosens when he walks in, how his face gets shady with longing when he pushes through the swell of the bead-curtain doors that fall in the foyer like lines of computer code. I think he aches for all that reminding it does, how it taps him ever so sweetly with callbacks to his days in the loose-lipped sixties.

Bobby says, "We gonna spend all day here?" and we hightail it back outside. The streets shimmer in a tenuous sun, the best kind of chilly. Both lakes bustle in the breeze, leaping out for each other over the bleeding heart of the isthmus.

"You'll call if you need to, yeah?" Bobby asks. "Or text? With the whole party thing?" His face is changed, voice balking from high to low. I know the phrase is beaten to death, but the only way to classify Bobby's brown eyes is to say they're blinding.

"I will," I say. "I'll probably stay for two minutes."

"That's a long time, Ted. That's a long time for people like us."

"Only when you're brushing your teeth," I say, and when he doesn't laugh I turn away from him, like I tend to do when what I say doesn't land.

"Just keep to the plan," Bobby says with a smile not even he could believe in. "Always remember the plan. And dial my cell, if you end up calling. I don't want you hogging the store line."

He lets me off at ten after five, and I step into the haze of a pinkish sunset. There's a chill outside that's sharp enough to shave with. A breeze ripples the corners of a hand-drawn flyer somebody tucked under my wipers, and most days I walk around feeling like I've lost something I never had. Happiness might be the word.

* * *

What a thing it was my mother said. I'll relay it back to Bobby with haunting accuracy.

We were huddled in the corner of a neighborhood bar not fifteen feet from the shoreline of Lake Mendota's chubby west side, not two miles from where my brother Ollie and I used to live. That first-floor apartment where we ruined our lives ten times over, and where we set about the task of mending the tatters back whole again.

The venue, I was informed by every guest there, is owned by my only sibling's soon-to-be mother-in-law. It's a leaky-looking joint, wood paneled and painted white now, planted at the bottom of a surprising hill like a ski-mountain tourist trap. Twilight beamed off the lake in silver gusts.

My mom said, "Everything your brother wanted while he was using, he found when he got sober."

What she meant was a loving, loyal companion (check). A purpose-giving job (an associate's degree plus five years of the sort my brother experienced nearly landed him in the *overqualified* category during his interview with Hope Harbor Counseling). And don't forget fun, creative, supportive friends (I can personally attest to their coolness).

Mom's goal, I know, was to keep fresh in my mind that the way her sons' stories have progressed is not the way they tend to unfold, these days. That mostly those sorts of stories fall off the page and shatter like ten pounds of glass.

We are all too aware of this, Ollie and I.

When we were scoring, snorting, shooting, smoking, stealing, scheming, and slumming, the plan was always to get clean. Ollie just chose to make every step the right step—he did the detox thing, the halfway-house thing and the sober-house thing, fifty-minutes-of-buzzing-bee-sounds-from-the-transcranial-magnetic-stimulation thing; loads of lithium; solo meetings and group meetings and family counseling meetings; music therapy and art therapy and trauma-confronting puppetry workshops on weekend retreats.

"I'm going to do it all," he'd told me, and he did it all, and it was the most immense rescue operation I have ever seen.

My veer from the edge of the cliff was slighter in nature, which makes it less stable, more reliant on pep talks from my boss, and less equipped to handle the way my people's eyes bored through my beer bottle like some kind of alien weaponry. More prepared, in short, for the order to fall apart.

But I continue, astounded always by my continuousness.

I didn't get the chance to say but six words to Ollie all night. He was busy with the crowd, and what I did say was congratulatory and kind. He looked obscenely happy. As did his fiancée, a wonderfully good individual.

* * *

Bobby says we're broke.

"We?" I say. "I just work here."

He tells me that's not how he meant it. It's the books. Numbers tending toward the red end of the spectrum. Cash flow equals inadequate, and the bank people won't stop calling, he says, wanting what's owed. I go weak with relief that our trouble isn't outside the law.

I move to the door, flip the OPEN sign to CLOSED. In case this is my last time inside, I batter my senses into taking it all in. The keys tinkling like copper tinsel, that thick dusty smell of the rug by the front door. Even the door itself. Why didn't I spend every minute of my life loving it? Weightless but sturdy, streak prone, the best door I've ever known. I can see the blue bulging sky and the bed of bristly dahlias and oh what a view: the scraped-clean streets and the parking meters hooded yellow with NO PARKING sleeves, all of it caught in a swamp of midday shadows, black little Rorschachs cast by overpriced apartment buildings, blotting out the awning of the Peruvian place I still haven't tried. It's always funny when nostalgia hits even before something is over.

"What happened to it?" I ask. "What happened to the money?"

"Piss off," Bobby says. "I didn't splurge it. I did what I normally do. We just haven't been making enough of it."

"What's the plan? Rally support for a landmark local business being run out of town by fat cats?"

"I've been open less than twenty years. We don't meet the criteria for that kind of spin, fuckhead."

I decide that my only goal is to keep Bobby from sliding too soon into bitterness.

"What's the prognosis?" I say.

"They've given me two extensions already. Maybe I can swing another."

"Optimistic."

"Very. Because there's no chance we're gonna make it up."

I decide to ask something I've never asked.

"No," Bobby says. "It's not my life's savings. Just my life's work. Do you think it's enough?"

"We aren't dead yet, boss."

* * *

Our first order of business is to adjust store hours, cut down on operational time. We settle on ten to three. Bobby tells me I'll still get paid. He just isn't sure how much. Or when. Or if my last two weeks will come up even. I tell him not to worry about me. This is something I've come across before. He keeps putting on this can-do face, saying things like, "Don't let this mess you up, kid," and, "It's going to be all right, Ted."

If only I could tell him.

It was the same deal, way back when, after the FoxHead bar manager fired me for missing my third shift in a week. I could tell by the droop in his face that he was afraid, trembling in the soles of his Chukka boots.

I'd barely been on the right track at the time, and in fact tried to make my way to a favored old spot that night. But my car wouldn't start. Its guts were frozen solid, murdered by the polar vortex. Ollie was the only person who could come and give me a lift. Supposedly that's called divine intervention.

For me, it became known as The Night. The crowning moment when I started not so much to build my resolve, but when I made the decision to do exactly that.

The gist of what I settled on was this: I would become normal, would expend extreme amounts of internal will and focus to become plain and nice and unassuming, the type of person with work friends, who took the rough with the smooth, was a regular to some charming waitress and always tipped her thirty percent and was kind, warmhearted, and funny and eager to cheer somebody up; a person that tried not to correct people, who made healthy recipes from celebrity cookbooks and exercised three times a week, a guy that was lovingly stern when a friend did wrong and called high school pals just to say hello; the type of person who remembered birthdays and milestones and wrote thank-you cards, who went on walks and sat on park benches reading dog-eared library books, who didn't waste money ordering useless things; a person that didn't talk too much and conquer a room, but wasn't overly shy, didn't bother the host of a get-together because they were sitting like a nervous stump, looking at their phone; a guy who scanned the local weekly and went to lots of fun, free municipal offerings, who paid for music and paid attention and tried very hard to be a good person, one who would never have more than three drinks in one day under any circumstance, and would never get high again for the rest of his life.

* * *

Our days at the store are squished. Bobby and I spend them in a daze of dreary mindlessness, threatened by debt collectors and unemployment, the general fog of our future. This makes them screamingly fun.

We pass the hours like men at sea. We try to fold pieces of paper in half more than seven times. We throw thumbtacks into coffee mugs from the far side of the room, do crosswords with our non-dominant hands, watch hour-long videos of people wiping out epically on skateboards.

When I ask Bobby what's really going on, what really happened, he doesn't have anything to offer. "It's just one of those things," he tells me.

Bobby is failing to live up to his normal self. Quiet and reserved, his politeness is beginning to rattle me. "Bobby," I say. "What's bopping around in that head of yours? Don't me and my fellow millennials really get under your skin?"

"Nah," he says, and waves me off. "It's the Gen-Z kids we should be worried about, anyway."

I do my best to bring him out of himself. I watch TED Talks on full volume of people arguing for universal basic income. I tell Bobby I'm thinking about swapping my pronouns. I switch the background of the store's only computer to a photo catalogue of species extinction due to climate change. Nothing seems to do it.

"Bobby," I say. "Hey, Bobby. What's going on?"

"Places close. People die. Birds sing. Not much for a guy to do except do what he can."

* * *

Ollie has never been to the shop, but when he shows up for the first time he's more worried than Bobby and I combined.

"I'm not going anywhere," I tell him. "It's a bummer, but it's not what you think."

"Romance and finance," Ollie says to me, "are the two biggest threats to sobriety. And you're in the middle of a financial problem as we speak."

"I guess—"

"Let me finish," he says. "You're losing your job and your sponsor in one go."

I tell Ollie I've never really thought I had a sponsor. And if I did, it definitely wouldn't be Bobby. "He's just my boss," I say.

"Let me set something up for you."

"If it'll make you feel better," I tell him, a really shitty thing to say.

* * *

It's more than clear I've failed to ease Ollie's worries. Because of this, I've been formally summoned for a family meeting disguised as dinner.

Word travels slipstream-fast in a twenty-minute town like this. It's hard not to imagine the news of my situation making its way to my mother via the beltline, downshifting up the on-ramp near University Ave., jumping off at Gammon Road to skip over the stuffiness of the 151 interchange, all to arrive at its destination two minutes' shy of the original ETA.

I don't have much of a defense to present. Ollie and my mom will have to take me at my word, which doesn't have the highest credit score. If anything, what they want is to voice their concerns as a team, in a setting they see as serious enough for the scene. I can't help but be okay with that. The kind of person who'd complain about being the object of another's concern is the kind of person I do not want to be. Sometimes I see myself as the opposite of a solipsist. I think other people are more real than me.

* * *

My mother's condo isn't far from the Lacy Road Library. On her second-floor balcony are banister-strung lights and planters clinging tight to the railing. Most of the flowers have gone gray and limp, the green sucked out of them by some seasonal vacuum cleaner.

Across from me on the couch sit Ollie and my mom. Dinner is finished, the table wiped clean. There is business to attend to and nothing's been left to distract us from it.

"Have you been looking for a new job?" my mother says.

"It's all right if you haven't," Ollie says. "Maybe a break would be a good idea."

"You want to stay busy, though. It's just awful, isn't it?"

"It is," Ollie says.

"We just want you to know," my mother says, "that we love you."

Ollie goes, "Exactly. We love you."

"So much."

"I love you guys, too," I say.

My mom seems to lose the agreed-upon tone when she says, "If you don't ask for help now, we can't do anything for you. Do you hear me? Are you hearing me, Ted? We aren't going to do it again. I'm not going to do it again."

"Of course," I say. "I hear you."

Ollie puts a hand on her knee. If there were room on the couch, I'd be crossing the carpet, planting myself there, and spreading down roots in the cushions. I try to muster up the best smile I can, a smile they'd want to buy stock in.

"I promise I'm here for the long haul," I say.

Ollie and Mom keep staring in my direction, not quite motionless but not far from it. They want to believe me. Somebody's thrown a switch and the wind kicks on outside. I suppose the only thing to do is stay in this moment of familial meditation. For them, my future remains uncertain; for me, it's all too clear. I wish I could say: Yeah. It's still here, in me, the feelings, the deep bleak darkness, the fear of falling, of plunging, but it's not here now, right now it's gone and today I'm the person I want to be, and while I can't give a forecast on tomorrow, I think I'll feel okay, I think I'll feel that it's all right for me, sometimes, to feel all right.

The paths of our stares carve a triangle in the living room. We might as well be in group prayer. And it stays like that for a few minutes before things begin to settle. Ollie and Mom and me. I'd give my arms and legs for the both of them.

"We're thinking about a May wedding," Ollie says. "Did I tell you that?"

* * *

I see Ollie again, three days' post-dinner, outside the basement entrance of St. Patrick's on East Main. The kind of evening people call unseasonal, a heavy wind off the lake that's nothing but a whimper when it hits me.

I rarely come to the Thursday-night NA meetings, but I could think of no better way to up my family's confidence in me than an unannounced appearance. I'm hoping Ollie will relay my attendance up the chain of command. He is a staple at these meetings, which makes it strange to see him on one of the black city benches outside.

"Hey there," I say to him. "Should we head in?"

When he looks up, Ollie's face isn't his. It's a pirated movie, bootlegged. His eyes are from 2011, the same eyes that looked at me after we'd blendered our minds on a batch of spice over Memorial Day weekend. The eyes I'm seeing now are the eyes of that Tuesday morning: vacated, cold. We knew a guy named Red who cooked up in his garage near Spring Green. Red's stuff made you feel unborn. Made you think you'd never seen a shape in your life. Three days on that stuff wiped our motherboards clean, reset us like we'd just come from the factory, scattered everything we knew about ourselves and pushed us into a swirling mosh pit of what we identified, even then, as a terrifying paranoia. It had us banging on doors both real and imagined, running down State Street with shoelaces as T-shirts. It had us starting over from scratch, really.

I sit down next to him, the metal bench uncomfortable, cold.

"I don't know if it's the wedding stuff," he says. His hands are shaking, trembling all over. "Maybe something else. No, no. I haven't. I haven't even come close. I don't need to go anywhere, not yet."

There's a protocol for situations like this one and I try to remember it. Ollie tells me that Darren, his sponsor, is downstairs.

"Let's go in, then," I say. "Or do you want me to grab him?"

"It's just the wedding stuff," Ollie says. "I've worked so hard, you know? Putting things back together. And now the puzzle is starting to look finished, and I feel like the only thing that can happen is for it to fall apart."

"And you would be the puzzle in this situation?" I say, hoping against everything I've ever hoped for that he'll smile. Which he does. An honest smile. Worth a trillion bucks. "Let's just go in," I say. "We can talk to Darren. Or you can talk to Darren and I can fuck off. Whatever works. Hey, man. Ollie. Hey, Ollie, look at me."

"I don't think I belong in there. With how I am right now? Fucking myself up over a wedding? What a joke."

"Seems like the perfect place," I say. "Made just for us."

* * *

Bobby's Key Shop closes its doors on a Tuesday in November. It deserves a state funeral in my opinion. Fanfare and bunting and mighty roaring cannons, gratuitous displays of grief. Bobby tells me he'll try Key West. "I'm old enough and fat enough to fit right in. You oughta come visit me sometime."

"Yeah," I say. "Of course. That'd be great." Which is what you're supposed to say when you get on the topic of visiting.

"Take care until I see you next," he says, and he heads off into the streaking orange daylight. Something straight out of a cowboy movie, and it's a sight to see. A sight made clean by the shadows of the city, black and blotchy but tinted bright, leaning up against the stretched-out storefronts. A sight that'll stay that way. Polished, clean.

Five minutes into that Tuesday shift, when Bobby told me it would be my last, I had to admit I'd had a feeling it would be. Something about the sky that morning gave it away: the gray of an early cold front sprinting in from the west, full of linty-looking clouds with too many curves and folds.

"The lawyer is coming tomorrow for a final walk-through," Bobby says. "That'll basically be it."

"You doing all right?" I ask.

"Are you doing all right?" he echoes.

I could see us going back and forth like this for hours, ping-ponging the question until our vocal cords give out.

"I am," I say. "Do you believe me?"

Bobby says, "I do. Would you believe me if I gave the same answer?"

"I would," I say. "I might ask you one more time, though. Just to make sure."

"I'd probably do the same."

"I'd tell you all over again that I'm doing okay," I say. "That I know I'll be fine."

"Me too," Bobby says. "I'd say the exact same thing."

We stand in a silence so total I could only compare it to creation. In the store is nothing but a tidal wave of quiet, a nightfall of hush at midday. I can't get around the fact that it feels like the city is listening to us, pushing its ear against the door, wanting to decipher the simple enigma of me and Bobby, trying to crack our uncrackable code.

The sun is shining outside.

"If you put your feet up on the counter again I'm going to knock your teeth out," Bobby says. I smile, giving him a target. He smiles back. And we sit there, just like that. Silent again, and smiling, heading toward the next thing, knowing who we are in this world, smiling and dying, smiling.

JOHN DARCY *is an army veteran originally from Madison, Wisconsin. He publishes regularly in* Conjunctions *and* Wrath-Bearing Tree, *among others. A prose editor at Noemi Press, he lives in Los Angeles.*

A String of Lapis Beads
Greg Schutz

He lives with his daughter at the end of a dead-end road, in a house he and his wife chose for its seclusion. They were newlyweds then; what they'd wanted was to be alone together. Wild with love: he thinks of those idiot bursting annuals, begonias and impatiens, he convinces himself to plant in the shade near the mailbox for no better reason than that she used to, dry stalks by the end of the season. But they were better than that, finally. They settled into themselves, settled into one another, and began a slow greening: marriage. Susan was her name. She died a little less than three years ago, in a single-car accident.

Dani, his daughter, will turn eighteen this summer. She plays volleyball in the fall, runs cross-country in the spring. One Saturday, tentatively warm, at the end of March, she sets out from the house with the bundled, smoothly shuffling stride of a distance runner, everything held in reserve. There's a trailhead a few hundred yards up the road, a public right-of-way over the nearest ridge to the Pisgah National Forest. On fair weekends in the spring, Dani runs the trail.

He worries about strangers. Anything is possible; again and again, the world has taught him so. The worst things are possible.

As she departs he raises a hand on the front porch, and she raises her fist in return: the gleam of metal there, key ring wrapped around one finger like a promise, and hard against her palm the canister of mace.

An hour goes by. The wind works cirrus clouds into horsetail sprays. From the next parcel of land, the Kuykendall place, their nearest neighbors, comes the ragged nasal roar of a chainsaw. And when Dani comes raggedly loping up the drive, he's out on the porch again, waiting. She could almost be Susan's double: long limbed, small breasted, narrow shouldered. Reaching his truck, she bends, hand to fender, to spit a white bullet into the dirt.

"Nice run?"

"Ugh," she says. "Rat king."

Head thrown back, she gulps down the Nalgene she left on the porch rail. Her abandonment at such moments amazes him. He remembers how she used to sleep, face smashed into the pillow, neck sweating, sprawled across the backseat on long car rides. *Down and out,* Susan used to say, and when Dani woke there'd often be several dazed, blinking minutes before she'd speak or even acknowledge their presence, as if she couldn't quite place them, or had come to question their connection to her, given the cosmic distance she'd traveled.

She sweeps past him now, into the house.

He's a veterinarian, a solo practitioner. *Doc,* clients call him, which is what he's come to call himself. Most days he spends driving to and from farms, south as far as Cedar Mountain, west sometimes nearly to Tennessee. Dani begins college in the fall: Tulane, in New Orleans, shockingly distant, supported by loans he's cosigned and is determined to pay. So these rare afternoons when he isn't working and she isn't off somewhere—when they're alone together—are precious to him. He rests socked feet on the porch rail, front door open behind him, faint music rolling down the stairs, the bubblegum pop she likes to listen to in the shower.

Later, in the kitchen, she smears Nutella on toast, wet hair darkening the shoulders of the green and blue hoodie she ordered as soon as her acceptance letter arrived. He finds her there and asks, "Rat king?"

"Mmm-hmm." She chews and swallows. "In the woods by the trail. All tangled up dead."

* * *

Not tangled but heaped. He learns this later. Dani's gone into town to meet some friends. After a brief, stony climb from the road, the trail flattens out for a hundred yards or so through spindly pines. It's his land on the left, the Kuykendalls' on the right. Every third tree sports a pink ribbon, Todd Kuykendall marking his territory. Venus is out, plush sky deepening into blue.

By the shed, she told him, so when the trail bends close to the pole barn at the corner of the Kuykendalls' yard—just before it begins switchbacking up the ridge—he flicks on his flashlight, combing fallen needles with the dusty beam.

It doesn't take long. Here are the bodies, heaped.

Rats. Twenty or thirty. Poisoned, by the look of them: their tiny, swollen hands.

Doc's brought gloves and garbage bags. He fills the first bag and doubles it within the second, hefting the bodies back down the trail, down the road, to his truck.

His headlights darken the night around him. Driving is like sliding down a wet, bright tunnel. The rural waste center is ten minutes away, a gravel apron off the side of the road, some Dumpsters for trash and recycling, a Salvation Army bin. Someone's leaving as Doc arrives, a dazzle of high beams sweeping his truck, but by the time he swings the bag into the Dumpster the evening is still. Just the wind simmering in the trees and the distant hum of the interstate reflecting down from above, a trick of the mountains, as though a road's been cut across the highest portion of the sky. He stands there a moment, one hand pressed to the cool slab of the Dumpster.

This still happens sometimes—dragging himself along like a swimmer in waves, up and then down again, careful of his breath.

The Kuykendalls are having a bonfire, Todd Kuykendall burning the brush he cut back earlier today. "Arthur," he calls, his shadow detaching itself from the blaze as Doc swings his legs down from the truck. "Hey, there."

"You put out rat poison in your barn? Coumadin?"

"What's this, now?"

He spent the drive over measuring out words. You can't just shovel the bodies into the woods, he means to say. They're still toxic. Anything could get into them, poison itself. A bad death: slow bursting of capillaries over days or even weeks, joints and extremities growing hot and baggy with loose blood, aching with it. There are probably still bodies in the walls Todd hasn't found, bodies in the woods Doc hasn't, exhausted bodies still scrabbling for darkness, concealing themselves, because the last need that still holds for an animal in pain—he's seen it often enough—is the need to be alone.

You could set out traps instead, instantaneous. You could just get a fucking cat.

But he says almost none of this. He bites the words back. Faces flicker in the firelight, pieces of Todd Kuykendall's wife and children, his grandchildren, his friends. Fifteen or twenty people in all, lawn chairs and blankets in the grass, a stereo playing the Ronettes. Todd's face swings toward Doc's, fleshy and whole, as if assembled from the pieces phasing in and out of sight in the yard. "Hey," he's saying. "You all right, Arthur?" *Be my, be my baby...* Above the bonfire, a continuous whorl of sparks disappears straight up into the sky. And how can Doc even begin to answer this other man's question? They hardly know one another at all.

* * *

Weekly at first, and then every other week, and finally once a month, his daughter's been seeing a therapist in Asheville. Corinne is her name, a tiny woman, bird boned, half buried beneath ropes of beads and the heavy scarves and shawls she apparently crochets herself from skeins of sparrow-colored yarn. Dani found Corinne herself in the *Psychology Today* listings, having rejected, sight unseen, the names offered by the school counselor. "This is who I want," she said. Doc was surprised—he'd have expected someone younger—but of course he made the call. Corinne has a smoker's voice, a rare thing nowadays; over the phone, he found this oddly reassuring. She sounded a little like Joan Rivers. He explained the situation, why he was calling, and she said, "I'm truly sorry," in a tone both brisk and sincere. A relief: they could go ahead with business.

Still, there's something in Corinne's stern, professional gaze Doc's found himself flinching from, the few times it's been turned upon him.

Sometimes he drives Dani to her appointments. More often now that these sessions are less frequent and, apparently, less intense, they make an evening of it: dinner afterward, maybe a movie if there's anything they can agree on, though she'd usually prefer to pop into the stores on Biltmore Avenue or stroll through the open studio spaces and artists' collectives that have pushed out into the factory buildings and warehouses along the river. Usually he thumbs through magazines in the tidy reception area until Dani reappears, but once over the winter she slipped away after her session—just to the restroom, she said—leaving him alone with Corinne.

"And how are we, Mr. Jeffries?"

The same brusque warmth as before, only now he couldn't trust it. He sensed her probing intent. "Well," he managed, "you know."

"Actually, I don't." She smiled. "Hence the question."

Later, he followed his daughter into a small shop strung with prayer flags, shelves stacked with odd implements, folded fabrics, and packets of powdered incense, display cases crowded with jewelry and statuettes in brass and jade, the air thickened by patchouli puffs from an oil diffuser beside the cash register. Dani ran a dowel around the rim of a singing bowl, coaxing a high, clear tone. "Dad, listen." But Doc was distracted by the music—if that's what you were supposed to call it—playing from hidden speakers. Over distant, gently resounding bells, a woman spoke smoothly and somnolently as a hypnotist. *Now you are wandering in the bardo of becoming. If you look into water, you will not see your reflection, and your body has no shadow...*

"College can be a difficult transition in the best of circumstances," Corinne had said, back in her waiting room. "Which, can we agree, these are not."

Difficult for *him*. It had taken Doc a moment to understand what she meant, that this was something his daughter must have asked Corinne to bring up with him. He was fine, though, he said. Yes, it was a big transition. No, it wasn't easy. But he'd be fine.

Corinne had prepared a business card. Inked on the back, in spiky, intricate handwriting like the prints of tiny birds, were names, phone numbers, emails. "These are good people," she said, as though he'd suggested otherwise. "People who might be a fit. In case you ever wanted."

What had his daughter been telling her?

"Do you like that?" he said in the shop. "Should we get it?"

Dani dropped the dowel; it clunked against the rim of the bowl. "*Dad*," she hissed, glancing at the clerk, who'd paused in the act of dripping pale green fluid into the disperser, "it's like a hundred and thirty bucks. Jeez."

Although she did end up buying something with her own money, a string of chunky beads, lapis lazuli, not so different from something Corinne would wear.

* * *

The possum pouchlings appear one morning, three of them curled together in the coil of hose beneath the spigot at the back of the house. Little Star, their tricolor terrier mutt, an old rescue dog, mustachioed and sweetly stubborn about nearly everything, keeps snuffling around, ignoring Doc when he calls from the porch. Investigating, then, he finds them. Tiny things, each barely bigger than his thumb, atop a pile of something soft like rags.

Dead, he thinks at first, nudging Little Star back with his boot, but as his shadow stoops over them they move. The largest even raises its head to bare its teeth, a mouthful of icy pins. Not rags they're lying upon, either, he discovers, but the body of the mother and four more pouchlings. The mother's been poisoned—whether from the bait itself or one of the rats, who can say? The other pouchlings are dead of neglect.

"What do we do?" Dani asks. She's brought her breakfast outside, nibbling one corner of the Pop-Tart, chewing thoughtfully. "We can't just leave them, can we?"

No. That would be cruel. But now Doc must consider what he *does* intend. He can picture quite clearly the bottle of pentobarbital in the locked cabinet in the garage. One box with needles, another with syringes. A call to the shelter to see about burning the bodies, as he should have done with the rats before. He'll have to do that anyway for the bodies already here.

But this must not be what he intends for the survivors. If it were, he wouldn't have called his daughter out to see. He'd have done it in secret, stowing the memories away somewhere—another locked cabinet, an inward place he imagines many veterinarians and others in certain professions must have, where things can be crumpled up and left to degrade in darkness.

Bending down, Dani offers a fragment of Pop-Tart to the largest pouchling, which hisses through its grin. Little Star, jealous of the offering, moans.

"We can't just leave them," his daughter says again, firmly.

* * *

For a year or so back in junior high, Dani kept a pair of rabbits as pets. Now the hutch Doc built for her is hefted up from the basement to the laundry room, lined with torn newspaper and old towels, an electric heating pad tucked within the towels. The heating pad is Little Star's, another sacrifice the terrier will have to make. She watches it go into the hutch with a shaggy-browed look, Doc thinks, of martyred endurance.

"We're lucky it's her who found them," Dani says. "Deacon would've eaten them."

Deacon was their last dog, a dysplastic old blockheaded Lab. He died of renal failure about six months before Susan. "Probably," Doc admits.

The pouchlings lie together in a fold of fabric. They look stunned, helpless, simply breathing. Occasionally the largest one stretches, tail whipping, as though preparing to waddle off somewhere, but it never does. All three are dehydrated, exhausted, perhaps slightly anemic. One by one Doc has cradled them, each little body soft as a palmful of jelly atop the chalky second skin of his nitrile gloves. With a pair of tweezers he has plucked off the deer ticks that must have crawled from the mother's cooling body, dropping them one by one into a glass of rubbing alcohol. Dani has watched him do this, brow tight, gaze fierce. "Gross," she said once, but didn't look away.

Later, he drives over to the shelter with the bodies of the mother and the other pouchlings. Win, the manager, meets him around back. "Poison," she says, letting him in through the fire door. "The bastard." Todd Kuykendall, she means. Doc's called ahead to explain. "People don't think, is the problem. Or else they think and don't care."

"Just get a cat," Doc agrees, the line he'd rehearsed returning to him now.

But Win shakes her head. "No. The songbirds."

She's a small, sturdy woman, her hair buzzed short, her nails bitten down, with a taut, flexing intensity about her, an air of perpetual judgment. It's easy to wind up on Win's wrong side. Opening the bag, she reaches in ungloved and frowns.

"Only four little ones?"

She knows four's too few. Doc didn't tell her about the survivors when he called, but now he has to. Otherwise she'll have him searching his yard for the rest. She'll be there herself at the end of her shift, on her hands and knees in the high grass, asking questions.

He and Dani are going to try their hands at fostering the other three, Doc explains, glancing away from the look she gives him, washing her hands at the sink. Of course he knows it's illegal: he doesn't have a rehabilitator's license. Still, they'd like to try.

"Dani's idea," he hears himself add, lamely.

"Dani's idea," Win repeats, in a tone of caustic amusement. "Tell her Flopsy and Mopsy say hello."

* * *

This is a poke, a reminder. Dani named her rabbits not Flopsy and Mopsy, of course, but Haystack and Clover, after the hutch does in *Watership Down*, a book she'd loved since childhood. The rabbits were a Christmas present, something she'd long claimed to want. All the typical pledges had been made: care and cleaning, lifelong devotion. Finally, he and Susan had relented.

For a time, Dani adored her charges. A framed photo in his office at the back of the house shows her on her stomach in front of the television, one rabbit perched atop the small of her back and the other at her elbow, seeming to watch along with her. Deacon would have been huffing and slobbering in the kitchen, barred by a baby gate and his own bad hips from unleashing whatever bloody mayhem he had in mind. Later, he'd forage the carpet for turds.

Things changed. The rabbits rarely left their hutch, which Dani rarely cleaned. "I'm *busy*," she'd protest. He had to order her to do it, threaten punishments. He tried to explain. "It's cruel," he told her. "You're being cruel." Of course this didn't work. Nor was it quite what he meant. But he'd noticed the rabbits growing strange. Not that they cowered from him like wild creatures, but that they couldn't decide. When he was the one to clean the hutch, they snapped at his fingers and one another. They jostled for his attention, then sat miserable and shivering while he stroked their soft fur. The soured need of discards: he'd encountered this before, but never under his own roof.

Doc has never known what to do with anger. It leaves him choked, blushing, shaky. "We knew this might happen, didn't we?" Susan said when he complained to her about it. He stood there, shaking. So Susan called Win, and Win came to the rescue.

Flopsy and Mopsy. As if Dani might've already forgotten their names.

Watch out, Win's saying. And Doc understands. Forgetful: that's what he'd meant when he'd said *cruel*. He'd meant it amounted to the same thing. He sees it often enough. After a week of wet weather, for instance, an old bay warmblood penned in its own manure finally steps from a rotted hoof as if from a bloodied slipper, tripping about in the sucking filth with the meat of its foot exposed. No remedy but death, and Doc is the one who'll be called. Of course there will be someone leaning at the gate to the pen while he does what needs to be done: the owner. "I didn't know," they'll swear, as if that weren't precisely the point. No evil intent is required. The act of leaving, of leaving alone, will do. That's how fragile things are.

* * *

The pouchlings are stupid, feeble, helpless in ways he never would have guessed. He mixes dishes of water and calcium glubionate syrup for them; they use these as a toilet. The biggest one bloodies its nose against the chicken wire of the hutch, scraping it back and forth like a prisoner with a tin cup, so the wire must be replaced with fabric mesh from the hardware store. He works in solid foods—wet kibble, mashed potatoes, jars of strained carrots and peas—but these need to be supplemented with puppy formula. He stretches surgical tubing over the nib of his smallest syringe, which they suck at until they choke, tiny nostrils fizzing. Their shit smears like toothpaste.

Where is Dani, during all this?

On her way out the door in the morning, wrinkling her nose: "Stinks in here." Or with a friend, taking a break from what is supposed to be an AP Lit study session, though the music and laughter from behind her closed door has suggested otherwise, the two girls cooing now at the little creatures and scritching fingernails against the mesh. The pouchlings ignore them. Or at the kitchen table with a pouchling curled in the crook of her arm, doing the real work of care. These moments are fitful, unpredictable, yet she performs them with absolute devotion. "There you go," she says, offering the syringe. Not too fast, he warns, not for the first time, and she replies, not for the first time, "I *know*." Ignoring him, continuing: "There you go. There you go."

Two weeks is all Win would allow. On the last night, they watch a nature documentary on Netflix, a new series, startlingly beautiful, produced at enormous expense. Little Star sleeps at the foot of Doc's recliner; the pouchlings, increasingly nocturnal, clamber about in their hutch. "What I heard," Dani says, falling across the sofa with a Sprite, setting her calculus homework aflutter on the coffee table, "is they had trouble finding footage without trash in it. They had to have this whole team out there picking up litter before they could film anything."

Where could she have heard this? Almost anywhere, possibly—she flashes through page after page on her phone far faster than he can follow—or nowhere at all. It may simply sound true to her, a matter of belief. The music swells. They're treated to shot after gorgeous aerial shot of sprawling savanna, with not a single speck of trash, not a glimpse of human encroachment to be seen. He wants her to be wrong, but fears she's probably not. He wants to know how such stories make her feel. Not exhausted, it seems. Not afraid. Her griefs weigh differently than his—maybe simply less. Drone footage is nothing like the swift sweep of a helicopter, the aircraft's shadow racing along the ground, parting the herds below. Instead, the camera floats along in silence, invisible, like the disembodied, soaring eye he becomes sometimes in dreams.

* * *

Carol Ann Chesnutt is the name of the woman Win put him in touch with. She's been advising him over the phone, scolding him sometimes: "Chicken wire? For Pete's sake."

The number must be a landline. Once a man answered, grunting a single inscrutable word. "Salvage." When Doc tried to apologize, thinking he'd misdialed, the man laughed. "Got it. You're the guy with the possums." And in a moment Carol Ann was on the line—her firm, patient, convicted voice with its undertones of amusement: tut-tutting, almost motherly.

"So. What is it now?"

The address she's provided leads them down an access road along the interstate. A Burger King sign hovers over a glassed and netted play area; strung pennants snap above a used-car lot. "I like ours better," Dani says, sitting shotgun, and he knows without having to ask that she means the children in the play area and the pouchlings in the towel-lined box she holds in her lap. She's in a sunny mood, skipping school to join him.

They turn at the promised sign: *Cedar Creek Salvage*. A steel gate stands open. "All the way back," Carol Ann said, which means they don't park in the lot out in front of the pole barn with its attached office. A Doberman lies heavily on its side in the thin shade of a sycamore, not lifting its head as they pass. A man in canvas overalls leans out the office door to give a curt nod and squirt tobacco juice into a Styrofoam cup. The gravel lane circles around back, through the ruins. Cars and trucks, tractors and vans, heaped appliances spilling their mechanical innards, the rusted gantry of a crane like a dinosaur's spine. Everything glitters: old chrome catching sun, the powdery glint of crushed glass. Flowers blinking in the weeds seem dull by comparison.

All the way back turns out to be a single-wide trailer sidled up beneath a stand of skinny pines. They park in the worn grass, beside a vintage two-tone Ram Charger sitting high on a lift kit— "Somebody's toy," remarks Dani, who's inherited her mother's wry appreciation for the hypertrophies inflicted upon trucks in this part of the world—and before he can step around the front of his pickup to help his daughter with the box, a woman calls out from the shade of the pines, raising an arm darkly sleeved in ink.

This is Carol Ann Chesnutt. She's not what Doc expected. It's a girl who grasps his hand—*girl* is the word that comes to mind. She might be twenty-five, broad hipped in jeans and a racerback tank patched with sweat beneath each breast and across a thick, almost babyish roll of belly fat. She has a pair of work gloves shoved down one pocket and a grip that says she's testing him, or is used to being tested herself.

"And these must be the munchkins," she says. "Well, come along. I was just putting on the finishing touches around back."

Munchkins. Come along. Such quaint constructions. But then there's her left arm, a crawling portrait in green and red and blue, no distinct forms Doc can pick out, just scales and fire and the muscular, rushing water of Japanese woodblock prints. At the back of her shoulder, distinct from the rest, a snake clutches its tail in its jaws, forming a circle the size of a curled hand. "Nice ouroboros," Dani says—adding, more shyly, "did it hurt?"

"My first. Nothing hurts like your first."

"But after that it's easier?"

It might alarm Doc, the interest she's showing. But he's more startled by the sound of that word in his daughter's voice: *ouroboros*.

Carol Ann grins. "Would you want it not to hurt?"

The enclosure is shaded by pines, steel roofed, screened on three sides. Old stumps have been dragged in, bundled branches, plywood platforms constructed as perches. Pine straw has been scattered and stacked in bales. Gaps in the stack form caves, and an old section of culvert runs through the stack at the bottom.

A midday transfer is best, according to Carol Ann. The pouchlings will sleep through everything, waking to a new world. Not that they're pouchlings anymore, technically. Young possums. She'll offer water in a dish but not food. She'll hide kibble and diced yams and thawed mail-order mice to teach them to forage, release crickets into the enclosure to teach them to hunt. She tips the box gently onto its side, facing away from them, leaving a small gap between it and the stacked bales. Latching the door to the enclosure, she offers Doc a level glance. "You don't need the towel back, do you?" And he realizes—another shock, though it shouldn't be—that the thing they've come to do has already happened.

* * *

An airhorn sounds and the runners set out, jogging across the open field. An eager few sprint off into the lead. Stupid rabbits, his daughter calls them. She'll run them all down in the end. But for now, Dani's lost to him, somewhere in the pack. He searches the flashing faces for hers, for her neon green compression socks in the churn of legs. A momentary glimpse—blank, loosened expression, bouncing ponytail—and she's gone, the pack jostling down to triple file as they approach the wooded trail, disappearing finally into the trees.

He knows this is her favorite part: elbows clashing, clipped heels, gasps and curses, the struggle to wrest herself free.

Together with the other parents and family members, he follows coaches from various high schools across a cleat-torn soccer field to where the runners will eventually emerge. It's the final meet of regionals, a week before Dani's graduation, and he's surrounded by people he knows, people with whom he'd say he's friendly, people who've greeted him by name—*Hey there, Arthur*—which is to say they're not quite his friends. Even Susan, who knew him better than anyone, mostly just called him Doc.

"Listen," she used to say, those first ecstatic weeks alone in their new house together, lying in bed. *Listen.* So they closed their eyes, stilled their breath, and listened to the house as it settled, the slow, spare music of nails squeezed by lumber and water shifting in pipes. And the longer they listened, the more there'd been to hear. Even the silence revealed hidden textures, as perceptible in the dark bedroom as an electrical charge—as though their presence together, their daily movements, had gently rubbed each floorboard and wall, generating these vibrations, this not quite imaginary hum. She rested her hand on his heart. He rested his on her stomach, where their little girl was.

First come the new frontrunners, a cluster of tall, skinny girls pressing hard, shockingly leggy in bibs and bright shorts, every mud-spattered sinew revealed. Dani's not among them; he knows not to expect her here. "They're made for it," she's said of these girls, with their track scholarships to Duke and Chapel Hill. "They don't suffer like the rest of us."

She's thirty seconds back, part of a long umbilical connecting the leaders to the pack. Two of her friends are running with her, all three in stride, close enough to hold hands. Coaches trot along, shouting things like *Focus! Focus!* But Dani doesn't look at them, doesn't look for Doc. Her cheeks are flushed, her ears aglow as if in mortification. Together with her friends, she follows the flagged path around the perimeter of the field and returns to the trees.

One more lap. The crowd shifts to the finish line.

At some point in the woods, Dani will kick free of her friends. Running hard, chasing the leaders—on a good day even cutting the gap between them—and emerging, at last, alone. Most parents cheer their daughters across the finish line, but Doc never does. Something in her face warns against it. Any sound he might make would be superfluous, and his chest is too tight to cry out besides. He just tries to breathe with her.

Afterward, Dani and her friends pose together, phones held out in their usual postrace ritual, a triple selfie. She smiles for the flash, her whole face crimson and white in patches, the same colors as her lips and teeth.

He confronted her exactly once about her college plans: Didn't she want to at least apply somewhere in-state? What about her friends? His daughter just glared at the question, glared down at her dinner, glared at the four walls of the kitchen, measuring the space for her escape. But Doc understands—of course he does. He doesn't need Corinne or anyone else to explain. To go where she isn't already known, where she won't be The Girl Whose Mother Has Died: for Dani, escape must be precisely the point. He's seen her studying these selfies on her phone, flicking and tapping, changing things. A touch of her finger and a reticle appears, framing her face, bringing it forward and smudging the rest. Her friends blur into the background. Another touch: they reappear. Touch again, and they're gone.

* * *

"Darling," he says. "Wake up."

A starry evening near the end of August. They're approaching the end of a ten-hour drive. South of Slidell, Louisiana, the interstate leaps out over the water, everything dark above and below, headlights and taillights floating in their windows and mirrors, all neatly aligned and so apparently still he could convince himself, if not for the hum of the road and the rhythmic thuds of the bridge spacers, that they aren't really moving at all. But from over the horizon a distant glow has begun spreading upward into the sky. In the humid air it looks more solid than light: a vapor, a fog.

The first glimpse of New Orleans: she wouldn't want to miss it.

"Darling," he says again, but glancing over he can see she's already awake, her eyes open, dully gleaming. She doesn't acknowledge that he's spoken, doesn't acknowledge him at all. She may have been awake for a long time already, watching the light ahead in silence.

* * *

Three more things happen. Three things of note.

He catches himself organizing his thoughts like this in the following weeks and months—almost as if he really had called one of the numbers Corinne had offered, as if he were talking to someone, a sympathetic stranger, for whom his experiences must be unpacked and arranged, presented as if they had meaning.

In truth, he doesn't know where he put Corinne's card. He's allowed himself to forget; he may even have thrown it away. It's not that he has no faith in therapy. He's watched his daughter, after all. The very first spring she planted impatiens with him out near the mailbox, and he caught himself staring at her long-fingered hands working gloveless in the dirt. She stopped what she was doing and placed a lovely hand on his arm. "Corinne says it's okay to cry."

He nodded and kept nodding as waves crashed over him.

Perhaps it's as simple as this: now he wants to be alone. Home in the evenings, he paces from room to empty room, Little Star's nails ticking along behind him in the dark. And in the dark, pacing, sometimes he puts things in order.

The first thing that happens is an email from Win, forwarding a video from Carol Ann. *You didn't leave her your contact info,* she writes. And then, at the end, *Hope you're doing good.* The closest she'll ever get to asking after him.

The video is in three parts, three quick clips shot by a smartphone in low-light mode, everything blazing green. Three times

Carol Ann's voice sings out: "Shoo-shoo, little munchkin, shoo-shoo-shoo!" And three times, a low-slung form trundles away, disappearing without haste or hesitation into an undifferentiated thicket Carol Ann has chosen, presumably, for its distance from roads, homes, dogs, poisons, guns. Three times the camera zooms silently in on some spot in the undergrowth rendered conspicuous by the fact that a possum is no longer there, a last-known location, before cutting away. The last time, it cuts to black.

He forwards the video to Dani, who texts back only *Goodbye!!!* followed by a row of little hearts. "The Possum Lady," he remembers her saying on the way back from the salvage yard—as though it were the title of something, Carol Ann's title. "You think she really lives there in that trailer, with that guy and the Doberman, surrounded by all that junk?" Doc just shrugged. It was more than he could explain: the things people chose, the lives they wanted, and with whom, and where. He offers no reply now but a little heart of his own.

Later, on one of his wanderings, he finds her lapis beads. This is the second thing. They curl at the bottom of a cup on her nightstand, as though she took them off one evening, dropped them into a glass of water, and forgot them entirely. The water is long evaporated. He lifts the beads out. They rest rugged, cool, and dense against his palm. He rolls first one and then another carefully between his thumb and forefinger, moving forward bead by bead as Dani used to do, until something stops him. The shape of certain beads, a hidden regularity.

Every few beads, the shape he keeps coming back to, is a skull.

And on an October afternoon, brisk and bright, when he fires up the Toro for one last mow, the third thing happens. For a few moments he isn't paying attention, lost in the rhythms of the ride. And then the grass ahead glints and twitches, a muscled ribbon racing along. He has just time to think *snake* before running it over.

A black racer, enormous, four feet from the tip of the oil-dark tail to the brightly bleeding stump where a head once was. The body whips and thrashes, and when he picks it up—not knowing why, but maybe just to hold it still, just to stop that awful writhing—it lashes around his forearm and constricts. Doc hears himself gasp: impossible something dead could be so strong. Try as he might, he can't tear it away. His fingertips fizz, darkening like matchheads. All he can do is wait.

Down on his knees, skin printed with scales.

GREG SCHUTZ's *stories have appeared in* Ploughshares, *the* Alaska Quarterly Review, *the* Colorado Review, *the* Sycamore Review, Third Coast, *the* Carolina Quarterly, New Stories from the Midwest, *and elsewhere. A graduate of the Helen Zell Writers' Program at the University of Michigan, he has received fellowships and support from the Bread Loaf Writers' Conference, the Kimmel Harding Nelson Center for the Arts, and the Fine Arts Work Center in Provincetown, Massachusetts. He lives in Chelsea, Michigan, with his partner and their terrier.*

A Long and Circuitous Path

Monica Macansantos

The Masters Review Vol. I, "The Feast of All Souls" selected by Lauren Groff

My first acceptance from an American literary journal came from *The Masters Review* in early 2012. I had one decent story, which was perhaps the first good story I had written for an MFA workshop, and decided to send it in. As a writer from the Philippines who had been told by fellow Filipino writers that Americans didn't care for our work, I had the nagging feeling that I had made a mistake in coming all the way to the US to study creative writing. Were Filipinos meant to make it as writers in America, when so many of my countrymen were telling me to give up my dreams and become a nurse instead?

The email I received from Kim Winternheimer describing how much Lauren Groff loved my story, "The Feast of All Souls," came as a complete shock to me. As the news sank in that my story about visiting a child's grave in my hometown's overcrowded cemetery would be in the inaugural volume of *The Masters Review*, I began to feel like I had been given permission to believe in my writing, and in my dreams. This acceptance gave me courage in what I was doing, for this was a story I had written in America, after my professors at the Michener Center had decided to take a chance on me.

After this, I found it easier to weather the rejections that came, for I knew that I was good, and that good things would happen to me if I just kept going. I took a year off after my MFA to move in with my parents in the Philippines and knock out a draft of a novel, because everyone said that one had to write a novel to become a published author. I was awarded a residency at Hedgebrook, where I wrote a hundred and sixty thousand more words in my little cottage in the woods. I found a creative writing PhD program in New Zealand that did not require coursework and would give me the time I needed to finish and polish my novel. I applied, and they offered me a scholarship. This, and the occasional acceptances I received from literary journals, reassured me that I was on a straightforward path to achieving my dreams.

I signed with an agent at one of the top New York agencies during my second year in New Zealand. I remember walking across downtown Wellington afterward, and buying Christmas trimmings from an Episcopalian Church's gift shop to commemorate that special day. I felt as if I had stepped through a gate I was never meant to cross, and that a huge, bright expanse was opening up before me, welcoming me in.

Little did I know that my agent would fail to sell my collection, or that I'd get rejections from editors at Big Five houses confessing a failure to connect with my voice. One editor would complain that my stories didn't possess the sights and smells that would transport her to another land, as if the country whose sights and smells I described simply wasn't the kind of place that filled her with first-world giddiness as she planned another getaway. Unsurprisingly, an editor of color was the only one who felt a connection with my work, while also professing that work of such subtlety rarely found a market. My agent asked me if I wanted to do another round of submissions, or if I preferred to take a break to reassess our strategy. I was in the middle of a new novel draft, and sensed that a completed novel was what my agent wanted before we moved forward.

A few months later, my father died very suddenly and unexpectedly, sending me into a tailspin of emotions that left me wondering if I'd ever write again. I had a dissertation to finish and a broken heart to nurse, and I didn't have the emotional bandwidth to worry over my agent's silences in response to my many queries. I count it as a miracle that I finished my dissertation, together with the novel that comprised seventy percent of it, in time for the deadline. I did it for my father, who looked forward to reading my first novel more than anyone else, and would have been heartbroken if I'd stopped writing because of my grief.

I didn't expect unanimous praise for my novel from my three PhD examiners, who hadn't read the manuscript until after I had turned it in. I thought that I was only capable of writing garbage through my grief, and to have my novel hailed as an achievement restored my faith in myself, and in the book. I told my agent about their feedback, and she finally responded with interest after months of silence.

I received her notes just as I was about to travel to the US to attend another residency, and spent the entire six weeks of my stay working hard on revisions. I sent her my edits and spent six months twiddling my fingers until I gathered the courage to nudge her. It took me two or three nudges before she finally confessed to me that she had lost interest in the book.

I edited the manuscript again and sent it out to more agents. An agent who had offered me representation in the past for my short story collection declined this time, saying he couldn't connect with the voice. I revised it again, only to receive rejections with similar wording. One agent said she didn't care for my characters, while another praised my writing before calling my novel's execution "a miss." I was in disbelief, since I had heard the exact opposite from my PhD examiners—could three highly qualified strangers who were uninvolved in the writing of my novel be so unanimously wrong?

I was angry and dejected. I had done everything right, listening to everyone's advice about publishing my work in journals, getting an agent, and writing a novel. I had left my homeland to write this novel, putting so much physical distance between myself and my beloved father in the years preceding his death. I had sacrificed so much, and it still wasn't enough, because I wasn't enough.

We often read about writers, fresh out of their MFAs, who turn a short story into a novel that impresses an agent, and then an editor at a major house. I used to compare myself to these people, asking myself why my career trajectory wasn't measuring up to this blueprint of the ideal post-MFA life. We forget that most writers have to take a more circuitous route toward book publication, which doesn't make them any less talented or hardworking. This is especially the case for writers of color who must subject their work to the value judgments of agents and editors who often come from privileged, white, Western backgrounds.

I remembered how the pieces in my story collection impressed editors at literary journals, and how two agents offered to represent it not too long ago. My former agent believed in the book, at least in the beginning. While querying the novel, I decided to send the story collection to small presses. While receiving many more rejections for both books, I saw an open call for manuscripts from Grattan Street Press, a teaching press based at the University of Melbourne in Australia. I sent them my story collection, forgot about it, and nearly fainted from happiness when I read their acceptance email.

This isn't the path I envisioned for myself the day I took a long walk across sunny Wellington to celebrate my transition into an agented author. But I remind myself that it's not for the fame or money that I'm doing this, but to reach other readers, maybe a young Filipina who's the same age I was when I received my acceptance from *The Masters Review*. Perhaps she wants to feel more seen in the books she reads, and needs some convincing that Filipinos can be artists too. In any case, my book will live, and that for me is enough.

MONICA MACANSANTOS *holds an MFA in Writing from the Michener Center for Writers at the University of Texas at Austin, and a PhD in Creative Writing from the Victoria University of Wellington. Her debut story collection,* Love and Other Rituals, *is forthcoming from Grattan Street Press. Her work has appeared in* Colorado Review, The Masters Review, failbetter, Lunch Ticket, The Pantograph Punch, *and* VICE, *among other places, and has been recognized with residencies from Hedgebrook, the Kimmel Harding Nelson Center for the Arts, the I-Park Foundation, Storyknife Writers Retreat, and Moriumius. She recently completed a collection of essays entitled* Returning to my Father's Kitchen *and is working on a novel.*

All That Is or Ever Was or Ever Will Be

Eliana Ramage

At Space Camp, I'd heard, you could take turns sleeping in a pod modeled after the real ones at the International Space Station. You could zip yourself into a sleeping bag tethered to the wall, strap yourself down, and close the hatch like it was all real, like if you didn't do these things you'd float away.

I was fifteen years old and I'd never wanted anything like I wanted to be gone. To Exeter or St. Anthony's or even Broken Arrow Christian Academy. Even to stay in Tahlequah but to leave for Space Camp in the summers, something to hold me over till college. I was an unfortunate mix of smart and disdainful and I kept track of the achievement test scores in my school district, my state, my country. I knew the Cherokee language immersion school I went to was mostly okay ("God's hand on our lives," Mom called it), and Oklahoma was pitiful, and Greenwich, Connecticut, spent more per year on a single public-school student than our mother had ever owned in her life.

"But they're not trying to save a language," said Mom.

"Jesus Christ, would you shut up about school," said our sister.

Mom said leave God out of it and quit teasing your sister and Steph quit smiling you're not any better than her go wash your face you're oily.

I used to get this feeling sometimes, where everything would stop, and it would be like I was flying above myself, watching me, remembering the moment I was in but from years ahead. It happened in moments where I believed most that maybe my life would someday be the shape I wanted it to be, like maybe I was doing things right. I felt that feeling so many nights in the fall of my fifteenth year, our sister snoring softly in the bunk below me. Me sitting up, shivering and wrapped in blankets, ordered piles of printed papers spread around me. Flashlight light waved over PSAT scores and essays and financial aid pages filled with numbers I snuck from our mother's pay stubs and bank statements. Whenever I started to think about how Exeter might not let me in, I'd switch off the flashlight and lean back and look up at the glow-in-the-dark stars our mother's boyfriend, Brett, had stuck to the ceiling.

I'd enclosed a letter for the Exeter people. I'd told them I was on track to become an astronaut, little shit that I was, which at fifteen meant I'd done very well in high school science and was currently harassing our mother to send for a Space Camp application. Instead she called Huntsville on her lunch break and heard camp cost $1,000 and said thank you and hung up. She spent the next four weeks changing the subject when I tried to bring it up, and then in March she sat down me and Kayla and said she had a surprise. Brett was in Gore visiting his parents for the weekend, and she said she wanted to tell us herself.

Mom said there wasn't money for Space Camp and it wasn't happening. Kayla said, "Got it, okay, can I please be excused," because she'd been calling it Nerd Camp since Thanksgiving.

"No, you listen," Mom said, "both of you. You're not going to *the* Space Camp, but you are going to *a* Space Camp!"

"Oh no," said Kayla.

"I'm running it!" said Mom.

"Oh *no*," said Kayla.

"Watch it, Kayla," said Mom. She said "Kayla" but she looked at me, her hands gripping the couch cushions under her, eyes bright, daring me not to be thrilled. I watched the clock above the couch, unwove the woven baskets on the bookshelf with my eyes.

Mom explained that she and Brett had spent the last month staying up after me and Kayla had gone to sleep, typing a proposal on the computer they'd bought together on Black Friday. "I even had coffee with an astronomy professor at Northeastern," she said, having waited days to tell someone that.

Kayla cut her off. "You're gonna make Culture Camp all spacey, aren't you?"

Mom paused. Looked down at her hands, raw and rough but sweet smelling from the bread factory. I used to press her palms to my face, used to breathe in the strange mix of rising dough and sharp-smelling machinery.

"It's gonna be great," she said.

We didn't say anything. Kayla stared up at the ceiling like she didn't care, this was my thing and she was above it.

I said maybe we should try again for Space Camp next year. I could save up. Back then I had a shaky understanding of how much a thousand dollars was.

Mom looked like I'd hit her. She was quiet and careful, opening her mouth and then closing it and then looking into me like is this really who you are. Mom said, "This was the best I could do."

So we knew it was over. That all that was left was to pretend. We nodded and said great, thank you, can't wait. We did the dishes, me washing them at the sink and Kayla drying them to my left. She played the Top 40 countdown on the radio and within minutes she was singing along—rapping, even—gone off to other things, free of the disappointment I would feel from that early-spring evening through to summer.

Nothing stuck to Kayla. The way she'd flit through the hallways at school, from class to class, friend to friend, it was incredible to me, and alien. She didn't seem to suffer from the same yearning that I'd felt all my life, not for anything but what was within reach. Later I'd tell myself it was better to be the way I was, to climb through life with a purpose in mind, a light to reach for through the darkness. But at fifteen years old, in the muggy warmth of the kitchen with soapy hands raw and red and the windows foggy and my little sister at my side, dish towel swinging at her hip, singing along with a woman I couldn't name, summer so far from her mind because who knew what-all she had going for her tomorrow, I wished I could have just a little of what she was.

* * *

There were ten of us campers and the room swallowed us up, every word we said clapping off the walls and rushing back loud and harsh in our ears. Space-Culture Camp was held in the school gym.

It smelled like boys, and the lights overhead glared bluish green on our skin. On the bleachers, which were folded up against the wall, Mom had taped cut-out paintings of planets and stars. She'd made them herself the night before the first day of camp, as Kayla and I slept, just Mom and paint and posters, the backs of which were once school projects and protest signs. She'd piled them on our laps when we got in the car at 7 a.m. that morning. *Moms Against Nukes*, on the back of Venus. *No More Budget Cuts to Cherokee County Public Schools,* on the back of the moon. She was never great at protest slogans. Our father had been some kind of activist. Our mother was one too, nine years after she'd left him. It would be another decade before she admitted to me that she found the whole enterprise exhausting.

Our mother was proud of her posters, her planets. As campers came in and checked off their names and ran like hooligans across the shiny yellow floor, Mom stood in her camp-staff T-shirt and leaned back against cardboard cut-outs of the planets. She'd placed Pluto directly next to Earth, like a sociopath.

Brett stood beside our mother, their arms touching. He wore a camp shirt just like hers, but with an unbuttoned blue plaid shirt hanging over it. Mom and Brett counted down in Cherokee, *jo'i tali sagwu*, and then shouted in unison: "Welcome to Space-Culture Camp!"

A skinny, brown-skinned girl with a thick black braid clapped a couple times and then coughed. I buried my head in my arms.

Mom smiled softly, and it occurred to me that she might be nervous. Mom explained that Space-Culture Camp—"for those of you who got dropped off blindfolded in the parking lot by 'your 'rents" (pause for silence)—was a very special kind of camp experience. "You're going to learn about space," she said.

"—and you're going to learn about our culture," said Brett, in Cherokee. Silence. He switched to English. "Now, we got two girls here from the Cherokee language immersion school. Can you translate what I just said, Kayla?"

Kayla jumped up. "Bathroom," she said, her pink plastic heels slapping fast against the floor.

Brett asked Mom to teach us what a solar eclipse and lunar eclipse were. Which—please, you had to be at least twelve to go to camp, and Mom really struggled through her explanation. Brett told us a traditional story about a frog eating the sun or moon—it's the same word, *nvdo*, which infuriated me—and how *that's* what an eclipse is. *Nvdo walosi ugisgo*. Sun/moon, the frog eats the round thing habitually. He gave us watercolors to paint pictures of a frog with a sun or a moon in its mouth. I painted a moon, all set to tell Mom that the frog was there but it was frozen and suffocated and dead and its body was too small to see on a painting of the moon at this scale. But Brett got to me first. He tugged at the collar on his unbuttoned button-down, leaned over my shoulder to pass Daniel a clean paintbrush. "I'm drawing the frog next," I said, "after the moon."

At Space Camp, you strap into a multiaccess trainer—like a spinning cage inside a spinning cage—and you rotate in every direction, no more than two turns the same way in a row, to keep your inner-ear fluid from disrupting your balance. Astronaut candidates use something very similar in training, only with a joystick, so they can practice stabilizing a shuttle on reentry if it starts to spin out.

At Space-Culture Camp, on day one, Mom and Brett put us all in the bed of a truck and drove us to the top of the low hill behind a Braum's. They brought out a clean garbage can with Styrofoam duct-taped to the inside, and tipped it over. One at a time we put on a helmet and climbed in. Mom did a countdown from ten—she was working from a limited base of knowledge and for near everything we did she had to say "blastoff"—and pushed us down the hill. Afterward, we sat in a circle in the grass and talked about how it had felt, and how we thought astronauts might feel in the same scenario.

"They'd maybe be scared at first," said the braid girl. Meredith. She liked to participate.

"You get used to it," I said. "If you can't handle the vomit comet then you can't handle space." I was proud to know that nickname—"vomit comet." It set me apart as a person who knew things.

Brett laughed. "*Doyu hadvneliha*," he said. It was nice sometimes, having our own language. Kayla had it too, though, and she rolled her eyes.

"Anyone else?" said Mom. "How would astronauts feel?"

"Nauseous," said Daniel. He'd lingered by the trash can at the bottom of the hill, before throwing up in it. Kayla had helped him out and brought him water and leaned her head on his shoulder during circle time, even though he was the one who'd got sick.

"Nauseated," I said, and immediately regretted it. Brett scrunched up his eyebrows and cocked his head at me, like he did at school or at home whenever I "got in my own way." That's what he called it when I was a show-off or a know-it-all or a bad friend. "*Agwaduli janehldohdigwu*," he'd say in the living room, the lunchroom, the carpool line. "I just want you to try." Whenever he said that, whenever he made that face, I felt alone, I felt thrown out the airlock, suited up without a tether. Do you see me, I wanted to say. Do you see me at all?

* * *

At Space Camp, there's a twenty-three-foot-deep neutral buoyancy lab for mission training. At the bottom of the pool is the pretend wall of a pretend space station with loose screws and deep tears and faulty supply tanks. You swim down to the space station and they give you a problem and you fix it.

There's an underwater countdown clock and a siren that gets louder and faster as you work because it's space and in space you're always seconds away from death. A red light flashes through the water, your white suit turning from water-blue to danger-red and then blue and then red red red, system failure like in Starfleet when the captain calls blue alert and it's dark and quiet and time to focus or else. And you're in your space suit, a hundred-pound mock space suit with the boots and everything, and with your clumsy, white-gloved hands you're trying to turn a screw back into place with a silver wrench, your wrist turning and your legs flailing out behind you, you're weightless, almost, you're almost there.

We didn't have that. Mom and Brett drove us to the creek behind Brittany's house. "Ma, there's a scuba park at Lake Tenkiller," I said.

"Camp is free," she said, slapping a snorkel into my hand.

"I don't know what you want me to do with this," I said.

"Jesus as my witness, I am doing the best I can."

I folded my towel neat on the grass and went down in the creek, keeping an eye out for sharp rocks and slippery rocks and snakes, making my contingency plans for if I cut myself or slipped or got poisoned. I felt that I only had about a decade or so to rid myself of every fear I'd ever had. In the place of all those old fears I put a slightly more honorable fear, which I called awareness and preparedness and disaster-response protocol.

Most of the group was downstream, not paying Brett much mind. John was saying he was Irish. Meredith said Mexican, like people hadn't been calling her "the Mexican girl" all week. It was a strange ritual, the listing off of fractions—you had to be enrolled in the tribe to go to camp, so there was more excitement in what set us apart. Kayla had asked our mother on the way home from camp Monday if Hunter was "full-blood or Black or what," and Mom said we were all Cherokee and all human, whatever that meant.

Meredith waved me over but I smiled and shook my head and cupped my hands in the water, pretending to catch tadpoles. When people asked me "what are you" it meant I had to talk about my dad. How he was all-the-way white—Scottish and Irish like most people we knew—and how he was dead, which he wasn't. He just didn't matter to us, or wasn't supposed to. Meredith spit water out her snorkel, dangerously close to Gracey's face, and laughed and called my name and I climbed out of the water. "I've got cramps!" I shouted. Meredith nodded slowly and ducked underwater. Hunter stared at me, forehead creased, like I had broken a rule, which I guess I had.

I sat with Brett. He had thick black hair and brown eyes and pink skin. He wore rolled-up blue jeans and a white T-shirt that said Cherokee Nation Tax Commission, which I asked him about and he said his cousin had given him as a joke.

"What's the joke?" I said.

"Oh, I don't know. *Uwohldigwu.*" It's just funny.

I looked down at our feet in the water, wishing our legs would look broken like a spoon in a cup because of refraction. It was the wrong angle though. I listened to the kids swimming, no more than twenty feet away but far-off sounding in the echo of shrieks and splashing water. The snorkels were thrown in a pile on the bank, tossed around and muddy with blades of grass sprouting out between them. I wondered if our mother would drive to Walmart and try to return them that weekend. I could already see her standing over the bathtub, scrubbing them down, laying them out on a towel to dry in the yard. At Exeter, you can take scuba diving for PE.

Brett turned his whole self to me. He was warmth and kindness and color. He was smart, and he thought I was too. "Ahnawake," he said. It was my school name, my Cherokee name, assigned to me off the name list in kindergarten since most of us didn't get one at birth.

"*V'v,*" I said, "*aktvdasdi.*"

"What's going on?" he said. "Why aren't you speaking proud in our camp language lessons? You and Kayla know all this—it's baby stuff for you."

"Exactly," I said. "No need to show off."

Brett took one foot out of the water and folded it under him. "Are you sure that's it, Ahnawake?"

Brett stared out at the campers and watched them for drowning. John and Hunter wrestled and held each other down, laughing and coughing and gasping for air. Brittany stood still, half in water, and stared into the woods where Kayla had disappeared. I spotted Meredith by the lone orange snorkel sticking up out of the muddy brown water, the saggy polka dots on her faded purple bathing suit, and the real water shoes she must have bought for the occasion. Lord, how she tried. If I hadn't been so stuck on keeping up with our sister, on being like someone so unlike myself, Meredith might have made a good friend.

I thought about telling Brett the truth, about how Kayla and Brittany had pulled me aside after the frog-eclipse activity and said it was social suicide to know Cherokee. *Social suicide.* It was the first time I'd heard the phrase and I liked the drama of it, the seriousness. I told Kayla that everyone at school spoke the language and Kayla said this clearly wasn't school and if I wanted to make any friends I'd tone it the fuck down.

I thought about telling Brett about all of this, about how I'd betrayed him and left him to scramble for answers and attention from twenty kids spread out on the floor picking the polish off their nails and snapping the straps of sports bras against each other's backs. I thought about telling him that he was the only person who understood the things I cared about like family was supposed to, who seemed to like me how I was.

But it was too much truth. I jumped up and hurried into the woods.

I walked in deeper, weaving between trees, my cold, wet thighs rubbing up against each other. My suit was loose on me, a one-piece with bright pink fabric pilling at my bottom, and the sun was hot on my back. I sat at the foot of a tree and closed my eyes. Remembered the mosquitos and opened them again. I wanted to yell out in frustration. I wanted to be somewhere else.

I slapped a mosquito on my leg. My thighs were heavy now, and therefore more often covered, and therefore lighter colored than the rest of me. The line where my suit hit my legs had hairs peeking through, a new problem that—shaving being itchy and waxing stupid—I would never learn to solve. I pulled my legs up to my chest and held myself tight, covering thick thighs pointy knees oily face. You can't be like the kind of person who cares about this, I told myself. I was better than other girls, than Brittany and Meredith and even Kayla. I was a scientist.

I heard a laugh, high and fast, and then hey shut up! Another laugh, deep or maybe just trying to be. I stood up and tiptoed forward, my hands folded over the tops of my legs. The voices started up again, soft but fast, excited. *Does anyone know? Nope. Not even your sister? Is my sister my keeper? That's not how that goes.*

The air was hot and humid, my skin wet from creek or sweat or some combination. Every step hurt the soft pink bottoms of my feet, not used to the twigs and rocks and cracked acorns strewn across the ground. The trees overhead made pretty patterns on my arms, the sun passing through them to print a hundred little leaves against my skin. My arms were strong and my fingers long, thin, just right for fixing mechanical errors or inputting data. A twig snapped underfoot and I froze, but the hiding voices didn't seem to notice. I was just observing, I thought to myself. I wasn't a snoop.

Observe, orient, decide, act. They do that in the Air Force.

I saw a foot sticking out behind a tree, a bare shoulder leaning against the bark. I froze.

"I mean, was she always like this?"

Daniel.

"Pretty much. She's like, barely functioning. It's like, we get it, you're a space nerd!"

My stomach dropped. Kayla.

Daniel laughed. He made his voice go high and ridiculous, like a girl. "Excuse me," he said, "but I feel like the aerodynamics of this dodgeball game are highly problematized, if you'd anticipate the coordinates of this dimension."

Kayla snorted. Daniel stood up and reached out a hand, pulling Kayla up beside him. They saw me.

"Steph," Kayla said. "I was just—"

I looked up at her. Something was wrong. Not just what she'd said—we both had a mean streak and we'd found a way through before. Something was off.

"Steph, come on," she said. "Let's talk alone." She took a step toward me and Daniel took a step toward her and she shook him off her without even a glance, like it was nothing. She kept her eyes on me and she kept talking, apologizing. Daniel reached for her again.

All at once I saw the way Daniel draped his hand over her shoulder, his fingers dangling a few inches above her chest like it was nothing. The front-tie bow on her bikini, loosely tied, the extra fabric dangling down at her belly button. She was still an outie.

"For Pete's sake, Kayla!" I said. I waved a hand at her chest.

"Shut up!" she snapped, gripping tight to her collarbone. Then, softer, "Please, quiet. Let's talk."

"Let's talk about this logically," said Daniel.

"Shut up," said Kayla, and me. Daniel held his hands up and took a step back. He ran a hand through his hair. It was brown and thick and wavy. No, *disheveled*. I wanted to hit him. I wanted to hit them both. I wanted to sit them down and scream all the acronyms I'd researched, like HPV and UTI and STD and STI. To scare them with all the things I knew about sex, like our mother back in Dallas with a gun held to her head. I yanked Kayla by the arm and pulled her into me, held her body behind mine.

"You know what happened to Mom," I said. I was looking at Daniel but talking behind me, to her. I felt her breath behind me, just under my neck. She was still shorter than me.

"If you think this is anything like—" she said. "You shouldn't let Mom screw you up like that."

"I should tell on you," I said. "You don't know what you're starting. It's dangerous."

"Just let me go," Kayla said, and I did.

* * *

I barely spoke over the next two days. Only Meredith noticed. "I'm *fine*," I said, pushing past her to the vending machines behind the locker room. She didn't follow me like our mother would have, like our sister, and against all reason my feelings were hurt.

Our sister could only see Daniel. When it was quiet they burst into laughter and when something funny happened they just stared at each other and whispered. In arts and crafts circle, God help us, we were asked to paint imaginary planets on the cuffs of felt moccasins. Hunter made a brown planet he called Poopiter and Daniel snorted but went right back to tracing Kayla's collarbone with a dry paintbrush. All I could think was that he'd touched our sister's chest—at the very least he'd done that—and I didn't know if I should save her or ask what it was like. If I should be scared for her or jealous. At night I closed my eyes and ran the soft part of my fingertips slowly across my collarbone.

We visited an elder in Park Hill for a pottery demonstration. Then Mom handed us Play-Doh and told us to make planets. I made a planet outside our solar system that I named Janus—we were still thirteen years out from finding Kepler-10b but I told Brett it was scientifically irresponsible to ignore the probable existence of exoplanets. Daniel put rings around Pluto like a jackass.

We went out in the woods and dug up wild onions, which all of us except Daniel and Hunter from Tulsa had grown up doing already, only this time Brett stood on the porch and yelled the Cherokee names of trees at us. *Nohji* and *ajina* and *kalowedi*. I still remember those tree words, but I can't match them to pine or cedar or locust and I can't anymore say "tree."

I thought of Kayla through all of this. At home Mom made Brett switch off the news whenever we walked through the living room, but I knew it was a complicated time for sex. The President had put his penis in a woman's mouth, and Brett's mother said it was shameful what that woman had done to him. I didn't want people talking about our sister the way they talked about that woman.

I wanted to see things with the same sharp clarity that Brett did, how he'd stand off to the side while we ran through our games and activities, while we painted the solar system on the cement wall of a gas station and while we practiced our closing-ceremony performance, an abridged "No Scrubs" in translation. Through it all Brett would stand to the side and point at things and say what they were. He'd point at a paint can and say *asuhwisga*. At a knife and say *ahyelsdi*. At Gracey and say *agehyuja*. Agehyuja, he'd say, not *agehya*. She was still a girl. We all were—Kayla, too. I hated her for leaving me behind.

* * *

On the last day of camp, we went to a rock-climbing gym in Tulsa.

Brett and the gym staff set up our activity, while Mom explained the rules. "It's like the extra vehicular activity simulation," she said. "Astronauts call it an EVA." I knew already what that was. How you hang from a rope outside a pretend-leaking ammonia tank outside a pretend space station, and you repair the tank with your legs floating out behind you.

"We're going to do something very much like that," Mom said, because the whole point of camp seemed to be to do our own, lesser version of everything. I leaned back in my chair and looked way up at the ceiling. It was popcorned and yellow. I'd always pictured the training facility at Houston to be made of mostly glass.

Mom said we were going to be in partners, and all up and down the rock-climbing wall we'd find index cards. "One of you collects the English cards and one of you collects the Cherokee cards, and when you have them both each you have to drop them from the top of the wall. Make sure to let go of the wall when you get to the top and stick your legs out behind you a few seconds, so you can feel what it's like to be floating in an EVA." Then, "Steph, can you get me a Coke?"

I ran over to our table and tore through her bag. It was huge and heavy and overly motherish. An empty box of Band-Aids, Neosporin, crushed pretzel sticks, an apple, a little tub of Vaseline half-melted into the lining. There were four bottles of children's over-the-counter medicine, surely expired by now, and a stack of unpaid bills she carried around unopened as if waiting for inspiration. I grabbed the can of warm Coke and ran my fingers against it, flipping through the bills as I sometimes did. Water, electric, mortgage, credit. Exeter. I dropped the can and it banged onto the floor. Hand shaking, I unfolded the letter.

"Dear Miss Stephanie Adair," it read, under the embossed academy seal. The seal said *finis origine pendet*, "the end depends on the beginning." It was some of the only Latin I knew, and I'd been trying to live by it.

The letter said, "It is with great pleasure that I write to offer you admission to Exeter, with a scholarship amount of $43,590. Congratulations! Your thoughtful application convinced us that you would thrive at our academy. We sincerely hope that you will accept our invitation, and inform us of your decision by April 12."

The letter went on for a page, detailing the few expenses my family would be responsible for and how to browse the course catalog and when to speak on the phone with my advisor. My own advisor. My own courses. April 12. It was June. I burst into tears.

And then I stopped. I ran my sleeve across my face and walked back.

"Where's my Coke?" Mom said.

"Forgot it."

"Huh," Mom said. "Well, folks just paired up. You and me are together."

There were four slabs of climbing wall lined up together, and our camp had reserved three of them. The fourth section was for the fourteenth-birthday party of a girl named Heather. It said so on the banner taped to her part of the wall. It was a boy-girl party with a CD player and family-size bags of chips and a glow-stick crown on Heather's twisted-back, butterfly-clipped hair.

I pulled up beside Kayla. "We need to talk," I said.

We leaned against the base of the wall, in our matching orange Space-Culture Camp tank tops, our harnesses bunching our shorts in a way that made us painfully aware of our bodies. My head was still spinning with Exeter.

"I know," Kayla said. "Please, please don't tell Mom."

"No—" I started.

"Hey," said Heather, swaying over to us with one hand on a flat hip. Brittany followed behind her, hooked to the other end of my rope.

"What's your shirts say," said Heather. She pointed at the long paragraph of Cherokee typed across our backs, the letters that looked close to English but not quite. I looked at Kayla and Kayla looked at Brittany. I tried to remember what I'd been doing on April 12. If the admissions people had called the house maybe, and I'd let it ring.

"It says 'camp,'" said Kayla. Brittany laughed. Heather didn't push her on it.

"So y'all are here with the Indian group?" asked Heather. She grabbed a bag of Cheetos and held them out to us.

Kayla started climbing.

Heather said, "Jeez, I was just being friendly."

"Yeah," I said, and began to climb.

"You're supposed to say 'on belay,'" said Brittany, who was belaying me.

"On-freaking-belay," I said under my breath.

Mom told me to climb faster. "Come on, we're behind."

I felt the grainy fake rock, coated in sweat and dirt and chalk. I pressed my forehead to it and closed my eyes. It occurred to me for a moment that I could unhook myself and just fall, the way it sometimes occurred to me on bridges that I could jump off of them. I pushed the thought from my mind. I gripped the wall tight.

"I know about Exeter," I said.

I felt our mother reach up, felt her touch her palm to my ankle. I jerked away.

"Oh God, sweetheart," she said.

"It's my life," I said.

"Not really," she said. "Not yet."

Beside us came the bangs and shouts of campers. The slap of a hand on paper and Hunter yelling EARTH! Another slap. Meredith. ELOHI! Slap. MARS! Slap. MASI! They were loud and fast and laughing, and the laughing told me that they *knew* it was weird, they *knew* it was ridiculous, and they were not ashamed. They were happy to act like this was the gymnasium back home, like it was Field Day at school, like it was the sorghum field outside church where you could run around after the service and act crazy and anybody who saw you had been seeing you your whole life. I felt surrounded by these people. Hidden, like no one outside Tahlequah would ever look close enough to see me.

Our mother kept talking. She was breathing hard, trying to pull herself up to me. "I left," she said. "Baby, I already tried that. Quitting school, running away—it was a mistake. I have to watch out for you girls, even if you don't understand it."

This was old news to me. How as a girl our mother had run away from Tulsa to Dallas, where she'd always wanted to be. How our father got her number from a Greenpeace petition outside a grocery store. How she'd been totally alone, estranged from her parents, her Applebee's tips taken from her at the end of each day. It took seven years for her to get us out. The first time she told me about getting hit—in her own terrifying version of the sex talk—I'd had nightmares for weeks. Now I thought, "Her *wildest dream* was to live in Dallas."

"It's the best school in America. And they wanted me."

I pulled myself up higher. She followed. I hadn't expected her to make it more than a few feet off the ground.

"I love that you're ambitious," she huffed behind me. "Kayla and I are ambitious, too," she said. "You can do big things right here, where no one will make you feel less-than."

"*Please*," I said, catching my breath. "*Stop. Talking.*" I let go of a wall grip and slapped my hand three times against the wall. I wanted her to really see me, to see my light skin and hair and eyes and to know that her worries were absurd. Years later, in grad school, I would clean house for a Mohawk woman married to a white man. One night she'd tell me she didn't really think of her own kids as Indian and I'd know what our mother had been trying to give me, even before I'd wanted it. I'd know, too, what of my life she'd been willing to sacrifice to give it.

Kayla shouted over to me. "What are you two talking about?"

"Nothing," I said.

"You got this, Steph!" said Brett.

"Kayla, talk to your sister," said Mom.

"I'm leaving anyway, in three years," I said. "And in three years I'll be in competition with people whose mothers sent them to Exeter and Phillips and St. Paul's. Whose mothers actually understand how college works."

"That's enough," Mom said. She was sweaty and heavy and awkward, her arms shaking below me. She motioned with her head at the wall beside us, at the campers chasing each other to the top, screaming out newly developed Cherokee space words.

"Kayla," I shouted. "I'm on you and Daniel's team now. Show me your cards."

Kayla stared at the grips above her and pulled herself up higher. "After what-all you just did to me?"

"I didn't tell on you," I said.

"Right," she said. Kayla swung her rope to the side and banged into me. "Whoops," she said.

Brett yelled from the ground. "Kayla Adair, that better be an accident!" He was unhooking himself from the ropes, stepping out of his harness and stepping aside to let our mother pass. She hurried to the restroom without looking up.

I slipped my hand from a grip and slapped Kayla lightly on the shoulder.

"Stephanie!" said Brett.

Kayla tried to kick me, missing when I swung myself to the side. I pushed off the wall, all my weight held by Brittany at the end of my rope ("God, how much do you weigh!" she said). I swung past Kayla, crossing my rope with hers.

The scruffy staffer ran over, blowing his whistle. "DOWN! NOW! This is how folks get strangled!"

Brett hurried to him, talking fast and low. He put his hand on the staffer's back, gentle, like settling a horse.

I landed mostly on the wall, but accidentally kicked Meredith's leg. It couldn't have hurt much, but she was tired of me being an ass to her. "I am *tired* of you being an *ass* to me!" she said, swinging her whole body into me. She pushed me into Kayla, who shrieked and grabbed my hair. I punched at her arms, fully off the wall and twisted around her rope. The staffer whistled again and again.

Daniel swung over. "You shouldn't have told on her," he said.

"I didn't!" I said, deflecting Meredith's kick. Kayla followed me, still clutching my hair.

Meredith reached to slap me and I pushed her into Daniel. The two of them swung around each other to untangle themselves.

"This isn't fair," called Brittany from below. "You're too heavy."

A second staff member had joined the first, and he flashed the lights on and off while he blew his whistle. "GET DOWN," he said, shouting into a megaphone. "GET DOWN IMMEDIATELY."

Brett shouted up at us, his voice cracking. "Please, stop! Please."

I bit Kayla's arm. She let go of my hair and screamed, falling against the wall. Her knee was scraped pink, bloody.

Someone turned the music off. The room was quiet, and when I looked down I saw so many faces staring up at us.

Brett switched to Cherokee, quiet and slow. "Stephanie," he said. "Kayla. You're giving us so much shame. I'm embarrassed."

Someone at Heather's party turned the music back on, louder than before. They talked and laughed and somebody called out look who's on the warpath and somebody's palm skipped fast against their lips, howowowowowowow.

Daniel froze halfway down the wall, one arm outstretched, forehead down. Meredith swung around to face the party below. "*FUCK* off," she said, loud and then quiet, there and then gone.

Hunter and Gracey were the only ones who hadn't heard, I think. Twenty feet above us, they drummed their hands on the ceiling and laughed, their matched cards tossed fluttering to the floor. "*Heck* yeah! We wooooon!" Everyone else was quiet. There were a couple claps, a loud congratulations from our mother returned from the bathroom, face washed, eyes red, her voice high and bright and weak. Mom said she had to deal with the rec center people and then we'd need to get back home to rehearse our song one more time and the second group didn't complain that they wouldn't get to climb. I think we all wanted to leave and never come back.

In that moment I saw my mother holding me back, so afraid of her own past she would force on me a small life. I saw our sister growing up faster than me, leaving me alone in the world. I saw the laughter in Heather's eyes, the confirmation that we were small-town and silly and nothing I could do in Tahlequah would be enough to make me matter. I felt surer than ever before that I would one day leave, that I wanted too much too hard to settle for the plainness of familial love.

Kayla was still watching me. "I got into Exeter," I whispered. "Months ago. She didn't even tell me."

Kayla cupped her hand over my hand, over the faded plastic grip that held me to the wall.

Brittany said to hurry up. Kayla said, quiet, "Let's go on down."

She swung past me, brushing her lips against my calf as she passed. She didn't want anyone to see. It was enough.

For only a moment I stayed, halfway up the wall. For only a moment I reached my legs out behind me and stretched my arms forward and closed my eyes.

People talk about wanting to be anywhere but here and that wasn't it for me, not ever, not at all. It was wanting, needing to be somewhere specific. Like I was all my life at a bus stop, reading the schedule again and again, checking my watch. I knew where I needed to be.

I breathed out slowly and felt my legs dangling high in the air behind me and suddenly I was wrapped up in thick, insulated material, fed oxygen and heated and cooled and protected. I could feel my fingers tracing along the rock wall and it wasn't a rock wall but an ammonia tank, a leaking ammonia tank and I was unscrewing the hatch, gripping sparkling silver tools in my thick gloves and I was a professional, my hands were still and expert and I was born for this. The crew was inside and I was outside, on my own, tethered tightly to them with a rope, a chair, another rope—in absolute wonder at the Earth below.

ELIANA RAMAGE *is a Cherokee Nation citizen from Nashville, where she teaches creative writing and works with youth in college access at a local non-profit. She received her MFA from the Iowa Writers' Workshop in 2018, and holds an MA from Bar-Ilan University and a BA from Dartmouth College. Her stories and essays have appeared in* The Baltimore Review, Beloit Fiction Journal, CRAFT, *and the anthology* All the Women in My Family Sing. *She is at work on her first novel.*

Eight Years in the Making

Jennifer Dupree

The Masters Review Vol. II, "Dancing at the Zoo," selected by AM Homes

I have a novel coming out in 2022. That feels so good to say. Especially since it's been eight years in the making.

I decided there was no better time than the start of my MFA program to attempt a novel. When would I ever again get the focused mentorship that's the backbone of an MFA program?

I started with an idea: a woman throws a baby out a window and another woman catches him and decides to keep him.

Everyone said it was a great premise. But that's all I had.

In my first draft, I wrote up to the throwing-out-the-window. And then, without ever examining the motivations of any of my characters, I had the next chapter begin three months later, after all the hubbub died down. When I was far away from the emotional center of the story. It turns out I have a habit of avoiding the hard stuff.

My wonderful mentor, Aaron Hamburger, encouraged me to stay in the uncomfortable place of the moments leading up to throwing the baby out a window. What would make a mother do something so extreme? What would it feel like right before? Right after? What would the woman on the ground feel—physically? Emotionally? Why does she want to keep the baby?

I didn't know. Aaron told me the only way to find out was to write it.

By the end of my first year of graduate school, I had a flawed and clunky first draft.

In my experience, it's no easier to write a short story than it is to write a novel. But it's easier to *revise* a short story because the story is easier to contain. I kept forgetting what decisions a character in my novel made or what backstory I'd given them. I kept notes, but not in any organized way.

By the end of my MFA program, I'd had the good fortune of having many talented writers look at my novel and offer helpful feedback. I listened to all of it, applied some of it, and kept revising. I signed with an agent just after graduation.

She loved my novel. She thought it would sell for big money. She sent it out sixteen times. Mostly, the rejections were vague and similar: "the market is overcrowded," "the novel is too slow for my taste."

My agent didn't want to send the novel out to small publishers. She wanted me to write another novel. I did and it was terrible. She was willing to wait for me to write a better novel, but I believed in the one I'd already written. She and I decided to part ways.

I queried thirty more agents and not one of them asked for the full manuscript. I have a whole bunch of clichés for how I felt at that point: gut punched, deflated, at the end of my rope. In short, I felt really terrible.

I went to a speed-dating style agent pitch event. I was so nervous, my entire body vibrated. I thought I was going to throw up. I didn't even get through my opening (extremely rehearsed) sentence with the first agent when she stopped me. "You can't have a woman throw a baby out a window unless she follows him and kills herself. No one wants to read about someone getting away with infanticide."

Unsure of what to say to her eradication of my entire novel premise, I thanked her. "Have her trip or something. Or maybe she lays the baby on an awning," she continued.

I decided to stop thinking about "the failed novel" (my nickname for it).

I wrote another novel.

I started a nonfiction project.

Eventually, I considered what the agent at the pitch session had said. I felt very strongly that the young mother in my novel *did* throw her baby out a window. But maybe there was a way to soften the idea, to make it possible that both she and the reader could hang on to the idea of tripping.

As a way of avoiding the hard work of the nonfiction project, I queried agents for my second novel and sent my first novel (revised again) to contests and small presses that accept unagented work.

I finished in the top six of one contest, which gave me the confidence to keep sending it out.

In November of 2020, nearly eight years after I started it, my novel was accepted by a small publisher.

My book ends with a contemplative scene at the lake—one woman sitting, gazing out, holding the baby and telling him everything will be okay. I could see the ending at the very start of my novel, but I had no idea how to get there. Turns out it was a long and winding path.

JENNIFER DUPREE *is a writer, teacher, librarian, former bookstore owner, and freelance editor. She has an MFA in Creative Writing from USM's Stoneoast program. Her work has appeared or is forthcoming in* Solstice, Front Porch Review, The Masters Review, On the Rusk, *and other places. She is the winner of the Writer's Digest Fiction Contest for 2017, and both a winner and a finalist for Maine Literary Awards. Her novel, "The Miraculous Flight of Owen Leach" is due out in the Spring of 2022.*

Comfort Animals
Travis Eisenbise

Behind every strong family is a story that left them no choice, and given the summer we had endured, a cat therapist was our last best hope for a normal existence. A few months prior, just weeks shy of finishing his senior year in high school, my twin brother, Jacob, died unexpectedly from an undiagnosed heart arrhythmia while napping in his room. That same day, after police and EMS shed frenetic energy throughout our home, my mother quietly smoothed the wrinkles on Jacob's bed, moved his unwashed clothes to the hamper, unplugged his lamps and television, silenced his phone, and closed his bedroom off from the rest of our house. That same week, and throughout the hot and cloudless days that followed, cats began falling from great heights.

The first, a domestic shorthair with sandy-brown fur, was found on the sidewalk in front of the library on McCormack and Main. Two men in orange jumpsuits trimming hedges for the city scraped its chunky carcass off the mottled concrete and tossed it in with the other bramble set to be burned and discarded.

If news of that first cat was reported, we missed it. We were occupied, you might say. No family has a go-bag for grief, and the absence of a fourth human in our home was as present as a finger to the forehead. My mother showered less frequently and allowed her olive-brown hair to tangle into a coarse nest. My father, a grounded optimist, did his best to carry on with daily routine, though I spied him many nights sitting alone in the dark, massaging the palms of his hands. Even Ravioli, our family Calico, showed signs of distress. He ate less, yet somehow gained weight from not moving, and spent his days either staring out windows or clawing on Jacob's door. We were not irreparable, just incapacitated by the sudden trauma in our lives. Jacob was here and then he wasn't, and that was a reality we had never planned for. In those early days of hurt we waded through each thick hour hoping for a distraction to ease our minds, to provide enough space for us to learn what new family we would become, but by then the second cat had been discovered.

It was a silky-white Birman, found by children at a local elementary school near the wall where they tossed tennis balls each afternoon. Upon seeing the dead thing, they ran and pulled their teacher's hand, screaming and bouncing until the janitor came and swept the tangled ball of fur and bones into a chipped red dustpan. "I kept telling them not to touch it, but you know how kids are," the school's janitor said, shrugging into a reporter's microphone for the evening news. "It must have fallen from the roof, from all I can tell."

"I don't like this whole situation," my mother had said. "Why do they have to cover stories like this?" She sat with my father on opposite sides of our living room love seat, sharing a plate of microwaved chicken nuggets and tater tots balanced on a pillow between them. To their right, in a recliner fuzzed with years of Ravioli's clawing, I watched the report with a morbid sense of fascination.

"It's not a situation, yet," my father replied. The ends of his mustache curled up, though my mother never saw it. Her eyes remained aglow with the blue light from the television screen. We ate dinner like this in the days and weeks after Jacob died, mostly in the dark, separated by furniture but connected through the conundrums of the outside world filtered through our screen. The ominous words of a local reporter vibrated over stock footage of kittens pawing the camera lens. "The question remains: who is doing this and how will we protect the animals we love?"

"That's two questions," I said. My father looked up, winked at me, and swiped ketchup onto his index finger. He held his hand down near the floor. Ravioli, who would have normally darted toward such a treat, stared at him from across the room and went back to lying despondent in the corner.

By June, reporters in towns across the country catalogued twelve more occurrences of dead cats: two Siamese, a fluffed-up snowball of a Persian, another Birman, four shorthairs, a Ragdoll, two Maine coons, and a hairless sphynx found split open on a fire hydrant, its lifeless body molded to the domed top. News outlets, frustrated by the lack of eyewitnesses, drew up images of what they called the Hurler. Pictures, some hand drawn, some grainy and pixelated, were posted on local social-media groups, stapled to telephone poles, and placed delicately under the windshield wipers of cars parked outside grocery stores and churches. They showed the Hurler as an unidentified man staring over the edge of various buildings, his face crazed with sadistic glee, the phrase *Save Our Cats* bannered above his head. The most egregious showed a loincloth-clad gladiator with a golden helmet swinging a cat by the tail. Small quotation marks around the cat's body suggested movement; a cavernous inkblot across the bottom frame labeled *OBLIVION* foretold where the doomed cartoon cat was headed.

The number of hurled cats grew by the day, cropping up in small rural towns and large cities alike. One cat, a husky leopard-patterned Bengal hurled from the fortieth floor of an apartment complex in Northalsted Chicago, actually killed a woman being led home from LASIK eye surgery. The irony sustained me and my dad for a time—she should have seen it coming—but my mother made very clear she found nothing funny about what was happening in the world.

One afternoon I found her in the kitchen alone, holding a cup of cold coffee in one hand and doomscrolling through social media on her phone with the thumb of her other. Ravioli sat unmoving on the kitchen floor, and she picked him up and began stroking the orange-and-black fur behind his ears.

My mother is a resilient woman, but she was also alone when she found Jacob's body unresponsive in his bed, and that is an image my father and I will never be able to absorb from her. Though she had done her best over the past few weeks to trudge along—working her shifts as a bank teller, buying groceries, helping me plan for my upcoming college move—in the closed-curtained haze of our gray home, my father and I became the sole observers of her sadness.

"How are you doing, Mom?" I asked, picking up her cold coffee and pouring it down the sink. She clutched Ravioli to her chest with one arm and lifted her phone with the other.

"I just changed my profile photo."

She turned her screen to me, and I saw an image of the four of us in front of our tree last Christmas, Jacob holding Ravioli, golden flares in our eyes from the camera's flash. Now, a yellow *Save Our Cats* ribbon snaked its way around the frame.

"I felt like I needed to take a stand. I just don't like where all of this is headed."

"It's not headed anywhere," I said. "It's just some dumb kids acting out."

"All across the country?"

She had a point. The growing scale of it all was unnerving.

"And Ravioli has been acting differently, don't you think?" she asked. "He hasn't made a sound in I don't know how long, and when I try to play with him he just looks at me like I'm annoying him."

"Yes," I admitted. "He's been lazing around a lot, but haven't we all?"

"I've been reading online that these hurlers are part of a coordinated effort to keep us all on edge before a more truly horrendous event. Some are saying a bomb or a cyberattack, but that doesn't make sense, does it?"

"Well," I said, "I've been reading online that sales of cat parachutes are on the rise."

She didn't even acknowledge that I was joking, just stared into her phone.

"Mom, please don't become one of those people who reads too much into things online. It's tough right now, I get it, but I can't leave for college knowing you'll be back here believing all that trash."

I leaned in and kissed her forehead. Before she could respond, we heard the front door open and close, and my father entered the kitchen. He taught physics at the local community college and carried in his jaws a visible pall of exhaustion.

"Kid tonight tried to tell me that this cat thing is all some sort of subversive government plot to distract from oil drilling in the Arctic."

"What did you tell him?" my mother asked.

"I told him that the only unfortunate thing happening here is that some cats are encountering the ground with too much force in relation to their mass."

"Tell that to LASIK Lady," I said. "I'm sure she'd totally accept her death given that riveting explanation."

My father leaned in to kiss me on the forehead. "I'm choosing to ignore that," he said.

"We were just talking about how lethargic Ravioli has been acting the past few days," my mother said, pulling boxed dinners out of the freezer.

"Again?" I said. "We never had frozen dinners when Jacob was around."

"Not now," said my father. He turned to my mother. "Whatever you make for us, we will eat it with gratitude." He pulled a few forks from the sink, rinsed them off without soap, and sat down to the *ding* of the microwave. A lump of steam followed my mother's hand as she removed the warm, damp plastic from our food.

* * *

Cats continued to be hurled from the sky. Some global leaders began to acknowledge the sheer precision and monstrosity of it all, but they had neither answer nor recourse. Three more cats were reported in just our small town. One landed on the rusted tines of a rake near a mausoleum in a cemetery downtown, another on the hood of a sky-blue Chrysler LeBaron outside a mattress store. The third cat was our eighty-three-year-old neighbor's snow-white Turkish Angora. My mother, father, and I watched through the blinds of our darkened living room as the reclusive woman stood on her lawn in a pink house robe. She towered over the sinewy, tuna-chunk-style carcass of her own pet, kicked it and cursed, then poured her morning coffee all over the dead thing.

"She's officially gone nuts," I whispered.

"Who can blame her?" my mother said.

"I confess," said my father, "I did see Ravioli out on the roof yesterday, but don't worry. He wasn't far and came right back in when I called. I'm thinking we might need to keep an eye on him for a few days. And, let's just double-check all the windows."

"On the roof!" said my mother. "And you're just now telling me this? I told you this was more than a *thing*, Mark. I've been reading online that some families have started locking their cats in the bathroom to make sure nothing happens to them."

"All I'm saying is let's just give it some time," my father said.

"Classic Mark," she replied. "Everything's fine. You know who wasn't fine? Jacob. And we didn't catch that one in time, did we?"

The moment she said it, I could tell she knew it was a low blow—beneath her. She backed away and walked to her room where she crawled into bed with her phone for the rest of the afternoon.

The next morning, a press briefing by the mayor of Miami interrupted our local Sunday-morning news. Behind him, a few bored police officers looked off in the distance while sad children in bathing suits squinted into the direct summer sun. Two very out-of-place medical doctors were texting on their phones.

There was a man, it so happened, who had finally witnessed the terrible thing, had actually seen two cats fall from the fourth floor of an apartment building. The man, whose shoulder hair could be seen sprouting through a camouflage tank top, recounted for the cameras what he observed. He saw the two cats sitting together on the edge of a rooftop and watched them clean themselves for a few quiet minutes. Then, together—without any outside influence or coercion and grossly aware of their own decision—the cats flung themselves off the roof to the ground below.

"We are now investigating these occurrences as feline suicides," said the mayor.

My mother looked to my father. "Now what, Mr. Has-It-All-Under-Control?"

* * *

The beauty of the Internet is that you can find anything. After a particularly long week filled with the personal stories of young children discovering their pets flattened on driveways and Ravioli's tour de roof, my father informed us that he had hired a cat therapist, that she would be coming in the morning, that it would be a three-hour session beginning right after breakfast, and to be on our best behaviors.

* * *

Our house, with its modest front yard, sits tucked into the end of a small subdivision, so when we saw a red sedan making its way toward us, kicking up small pebbles, my father announced for us to get ready. I found Ravioli lying outside Jacob's bedroom door, scooped him up in my arms like a sack of warm flour, and carried him back to the living room where my mother, father, and I waited to see what fresh uncertainty we had unleashed upon ourselves.

From the sedan, a woman. Her charcoal-black hair was pulled into a tight ponytail with flat-cut bangs. She wore dark-rimmed glasses too large for her face, a red scarf tied tight around her neck, a bouncy blue skirt with white polka dots, and saddle-oxford shoes strapped over knee-length socks.

"She looks like she's trying to rockabilly back to the fifties," my mom said, who had worn the same floral blouse for the last five days and had no standing to question the fashion choices of others.

"No judgments, Annette," my dad said. "You promised."

I placed Ravioli in the center of the living room where he just stared at a snag in the gingham carpet. My mother patted the open spot next to her on the love seat, and we both forced an interested look as my father opened the door.

The therapist entered, placed an index finger to her lips, and made eye contact with each of us separately. We were to remain quiet, that was clear. She rolled in a pink suitcase, righted it next to the door, and walked deliberately into our living room, her arms flat against her body, fully erect, like an Easter Island statue sliding across sand.

When she reached Ravioli, she lowered down to the floor, her chin resting on the carpet like one might search for ants in the grass. Ravioli leaned forward on his stomach, sniffed the therapist's face, and touched his paw playfully to her nose.

My mother, assuming it was okay to speak again, leaned forward and said, "You know, he's not engaged us for weeks, so the fact that he's responding this way—"

"Shhh," said the therapist. She motioned for us to get on the floor, and we circled around Ravioli on our bellies, our legs extended out like spokes on a human wheel, our noses practically touching. Ravioli, enjoying the sudden attention, pawed each of us.

"This is good," said the therapist. "This is very good." She extended her hand and stroked the orange-and-black fur on Ravioli's back, then petted each of us on our shoulders. My mother recoiled at the touch of a stranger.

"My name is Sara," she said while standing. "I'm a licensed cat therapist, and I'm so glad you allowed me into your home today."

My father, standing, said, "I'm Mark. This is my wife, Annette, and my son, Caleb."

"Nice to meet you all." Sara said. "Shall we?"

She pulled a chair from the kitchen and had my mother, father, and me squeeze together on the love seat underneath the window that looks out into our front yard. She picked up Ravioli, placed him gently on her lap, stroked his back softly.

"I'm here for Ravioli, of course, but I want to make very clear that my research has shown cats thrive on and adapt to the general vibe of their surroundings, most specifically to the family with which they live."

"What's that supposed to mean?" my mom asked.

"Annette, don't be rude," said my father.

"She's conflating *research* with *general vibes*, Mark."

Sara kept her cool. She spoke slowly, but with a confidence that swept anxiety from the room. "Cats and humans have evolved together for thousands of years, Annette. They were once thought of as carriers of disease, envoys of the devil, but then again the Egyptians thought they protected their most-revered god, who was born and died with each rising and setting of the sun. If you want me to leave, I totally understand, but there is real value to be found here."

"Cats also keep mice away," I said.

Sara pointed a finger at me. "I like you already," she said.

"Stay," said my mother. "I'm sorry. It's just a lot right now."

"I understand," said Sara. "How about you start us off then, Annette. Tell me why I'm here."

My mother pointed to the window. "It makes no sense, what's going on out there, and my husband and son don't seem to be worried about it at all. Ravioli is a shell of his former self, and just last week Mark saw him wandering around aimlessly on the roof."

Sara nodded sympathetically, then turned to my father.

"We're all a bit on edge," he said. "We lost our son Jacob a couple of months ago. Quite unexpectedly, actually. Caleb, here, is going to college soon. Ravioli hasn't been himself, and who the hell knows what's happening out there."

"It was two months and thirteen days," my mother said. "Since Jacob. Not that anyone cares to count."

"We care, Mom," I said. "It's just we don't go around announcing it every day."

My father leaned toward Sara. "I think it's important for you to know that Ravioli is technically Jacob's cat."

It was true. Ravioli was the reward for Jacob becoming potty trained, though a full year after me. My mother and father had told us many times how they had followed Jacob around the house completely exasperated by buying diapers for a boy nearly four when, one random Tuesday while watching cartoons as a family, Jacob stood up and walked on his own into the hall bathroom. The next day, they crammed a cardboard box between Jacob and me in the backseat of our family's station wagon. We drove four towns over, passing rolling green mountains, and returned to our home with a mewing ball of orange-and-black fur. Jacob named the cat Ravioli after the dinner we had that night, with pasta and sauce made from scratch and tossed together with Parmesan in a giant bowl.

"This is all very helpful, I assure you," Sara said. She placed Ravioli back down in the middle of the floor. "Cat therapy consists of three therapeutic human-cat exercises designed to build empathy, conceptualize barriers, and adapt to new realities." She unzipped her suitcase just enough to pull out a cloth bag and extracted a handful of marble-sized cotton balls. "If Ravioli was Jacob's cat, it means he is experiencing loss and grief just like the three of you. I think it would be helpful for me to better understand what he's going through, both emotionally and physically. I'd like you to go around and tell me something you remember about Jacob. Then, each time, pop one of these into your mouth."

"Hair balls," I said.

"I'm definitely not doing that," said my mother.

"Come now, Annette. Sara has very positive reviews."

"There's a reasonable limit, Mark."

"We don't push anyone to do anything they don't want to," said Sara. "Mark, Caleb, you take the cotton balls. Annette, you can participate without them."

"Thank you," said my mother.

"I'll start," my father said. "When we got Ravioli, I remember how happy he and Caleb were. Annette was so patient teaching the boys how to take care of him." He placed a cotton ball onto his tongue and closed his mouth.

"Jacob was my twin," I said. "Without him around, I'm not sure if I'm a twin anymore? A wife becomes a widow. A child becomes an orphan. But, what am I now?" I put a cotton ball into my mouth.

"Oh, honey," my mother said, reaching her hand to my knee. "You're our son. Nothing changes that." She turned to Sara and continued. "Jacob did this thing with his feet where he pulled his toenails off with his bare fingers. I found them all over the house when he was alive, and sometimes I still find them."

"Gross, Mom. Why would you want to remember that?"

"No judgments, Caleb," said Sara. "Every memory of Jacob is valid."

We continued with the exercise. I confessed that I knew Jacob had once kissed a girl in middle school. She bit the inside of his mouth and, though his lip puffed up in a noticeable red welt, he lied and told my mom and dad he'd been stung by a wasp. My mother missed the times when Jacob was sick and, while she never took pleasure in a temperature or an upset stomach, she missed knowing she was needed. Jacob hit puberty before I did. He was obsessed with eating grapefruits. He was taller than me by half an inch. He once drove my father home from the dentist even though he didn't have a license.

After a few minutes, our mouths stuffed, my father and I sounded more like walruses than humans.

"Jay-koob spwed maynaze in hiss hawr fo Hawoweeen," I said.

"I wemember tha," my father said, struggling to swallow. "Wen he waaaz gowing twiker tweeting as ah zowmbie."

My mother laughed, then turned to Sara and spoke for my father, who had beads of spit dribbling down his chin.

"Jacob was only nine or ten at the time and was adamant about being a zombie," she said. "He had ripped his clothes into tatters, drawn lines on his face in Sharpie, rubbed mayonnaise all through his hair to the point it was dripping down his face. But he got ready far too early—poor thing—hours before it would get dark enough for walking around the neighborhood. Mark and I laughed so hard. He just roamed the house wiping gobs of fat from his eyes, and Ravioli kept jumping up on him trying to lick his hair. He was so pathetic, but so cute."

I laughed and inhaled so suddenly a cotton ball lodged deep in my throat. For a brief moment, I played it cool, passed it off as just a hiccup and tried again to swallow, my mouth as dry as desert air. As Sara waited for me to speak, black circles narrowed my field of vision, and I began to choke and heave. Sara, unfazed, motioned for me to stand. She moved behind me, wrapped her arms around my waist. A quick thrust followed by a stern whack on my back, and a clump of wet cotton flew in front of us, landing on the carpet. My father spit out his cotton balls, gasped and coughed. My mother's face seemed to say, *I told you so.*

"Fantastic!" Sara said.

"Except my son almost choked," said my mother.

Sara just smiled and walked back to her chair in the center of the room. She handed me tissues to wipe my face.

"Jacob was a different human to each of you—a son, a brother, and, for Ravioli, a friend. It's good to take this time. Not only for Ravioli, but for you as well."

"That's something we haven't done," my mother admitted. "There hasn't been any time to just sit and figure things out."

Sara nodded her head in agreement. "Life doesn't stop," she said. "It just keeps piling up on us, doesn't it? The thing about cat therapy is to let that go, at least for these few hours we have together, and allow yourselves to see the world in a new way." She turned to my father. "Mark, I'd like you to come down here to the middle of the floor and lead our next exercise. I'd like for you to act like Ravioli did while Jacob was alive. How did he interact with you all during happier times?"

"I don't understand why we're doing all this and Ravioli isn't," my mother said.

"Part of our work today," said Sara, "is not only acknowledging, but also accepting that someone or something is missing in Ravioli's life, and to do that it's important to get into his head a little bit.

Since Ravioli can't talk—" Sara paused and looked at my father. "Right here, Mark. It's not a trap. Just right here, in the middle of the floor is fine."

My father looked to my mother who just shrugged. "This was your idea," she said, and waved her arm to the floor. My father stood from the love seat.

"No, no," said Sara. "Not like that. Cats don't stand."

My father sat back down. He waited a moment, his face tense with thought, then proceeded to fall forward onto the floor, landing first on his hands and then his knees. He rolled over onto his back, lifted his arms, and began swatting the air.

"Ravioli would—"

"No talking," Sara hissed. "Ravioli cannot talk. If you want to communicate with us, do so as he would."

My father shrugged his shoulders and rolled over onto his stomach facing both my mother and me. He brought the back of his palm to his mouth and licked it, moving his hand behind his ears. He crouched and shimmied forward to the love seat where I sat, jumped up and landed near my legs. He placed his head in my lap and rolled over, exposing his stomach.

"Excellent," said Sara. "Caleb, please rub your father's belly."

When I reached my hand to my father's midsection, he snapped and hissed. His fingernails cut across my hand, leaving a small scratch.

"What the hell, Dad?"

"Yes," said Sara. "This is all very good. Caleb, what will you do now? What is your father telling you?"

My mother leaned over to me. "Honey, Ravioli likes his scratches behind the ears, like this." She gently moved aside my father's hair with her fingers and grazed her nails on his skin. I did the same, rubbing my father's neck as he closed his eyes. By this time he had scooted his body completely flat across our laps. He curled up his arms and sank deeper into us.

Growing up, our family had a bit of a Saturday-morning routine involving my father making pancakes. Jacob and I woke early and watched cartoons at half-volume waiting patiently for my mother to come stumbling out of her bedroom, rubbing her eyes and brushing stray hair out of her face. Her appearance set off a chain of events leading to breakfast. We'd stand, abandoning the television, and follow her back to my parents' bedroom door. Inside, the dark room smelled musty and sour, dense with body odor, but it was our family's funk and it ignited in us muffled giggles of excitement. She lifted us each onto the bed, where my father slept on his side, covers at his waist, snoring. My mother held up three fingers, then two, then one, and Jacob and I carefully placed our pajama-padded feet onto my father's exposed back. At zero, we pushed. A great *unngphf* from my father unleashed our pent-up energy, and we exploded with laughter and shrieking. "Get up! It's pancake time!" My mother cheered us on, "Harder, boys!" as my father's body slowly rolled over. Ravioli, new to our family at the time, jumped and dashed around, intrigued by the commotion. Inching forward on our rears, the sheets bunching around us in small waves, we pushed my father's dead weight closer and closer to the edge of the bed. We were hysterical.

Years later, as teenagers, we figured out that my father was in on it the whole time, that he was already awake before we even got positioned in the bed. "You were barely five," my mother said. "Did you really think the two of you could push a 200-pound man out of bed?" Jacob and I looked at each other for a moment. "Of course we did," he said. I can't remember when we stopped the routine, at which age we just figured out how to make our own pancakes while my parents slept in, but at least for a beautiful time there the weekends began with all of us in a mass on the floor, feet in each other's faces, hair in our eyes and mouths, unwashed bodies emitting our family's early morning stink, laughing ceaselessly.

Back on the love seat, with my father meowing in my lap and my mother caressing him softly behind the ears, we inched closer to that deep, collective muscle memory coursing through our veins. It feels ridiculous to admit this, especially on the cusp of adulthood in an uncertain world, but after a few minutes of lolling around together on the love seat, my father began to purr.

"This is good," said Sara. "Annette, tell me how you feel."

"Silly," said my mom. "But happier. I haven't thought about those damn cats falling for a few minutes. That's a first."

"And if I showed you this, how might you feel?" Sara held her phone screen out to us. "It seems there's been a mass bridge jump-off in Norway, hundreds of cats right onto a highway and a mass pileup of cars. Ouch."

"You aren't fazed by any of this, are you?" my dad said, righting himself on the couch and readjusting his shirt.

"Mark, the most fulfilled life is one lived in recognition of its limits. Can we change anything in Norway right now? No. Can we get Ravioli back to his normal self? Yes. Can we bring Jacob back? No. Can I change the fact that if I use the bathroom, I won't be so uncomfortable right now? Yes. Conceptualize the problem. Change your reality."

"Caleb, go show Sara where the bathroom is."

I stood and walked Sara down the hall. When she attempted to open Jacob's door, I stopped her. "My mom might hate you if you open that door," I said. "That's Jacob's room. We haven't been in there for months."

"Two months and thirteen days," she said, and slipped across the hall into the bathroom.

* * *

Back in the living room, Sara bent down and unlatched her pink suitcase with an easy click. Ravioli, curious, walked over and rubbed against it, arching his back and raising his tail. Sara reached in and pulled out an armful-sized wad of multicolored fur, doubled over on itself. One by one she pulled apart human-sized cat suits, each meticulously made with glistening, wispy fur. To my father, she handed the tabby with its orange-and-white. To my mother, an all-black suit with emerald-green eyes. To me, a hairless skin the color of Pepto-Bismol.

"Hairless cats are actually quite prized in many places in the world," she said in obvious reaction to my bitter face. Then, turning to us all, "I'd like for each of you to put these on."

We stepped inside the cat fur and did our best to balance while holding on to furniture. The suits were warm and hugged our bodies. I watched my father hop around getting into his suit until he was half-cat, half-man. My mother disappeared quickly inside her cat's black fur. Sara came around and zipped us up in the back, and I shimmied my shoulders to allow the top of my pink skin to close as she flipped the cat's mask over my eyes. The head of the catsuit moved with the contours of my face, and the air—through the vents of the cat whiskers—was far more intense; I could smell the fine fur of my mother's and father's suits, the lint in between our new claws, the unwashed feline sweetness of Ravioli. I couldn't help myself. I got on the floor, on all fours, and sniffed the layered richness of the carpet.

From her suitcase Sara pulled a dowel with a ball of red feathers attached to a string. My dad noticed it first and took a swat at it with his right front paw. She jerked it just out of his reach and said, "Follow me."

My father turned his cat face to my mother. "I love you," he mumbled.

"Shhh," said Sara. "You are cats now."

"Meow," my father said, and forcefully rubbed his body up against my mother. Her mask muffled the sound of giggles.

Sara bounced the toy in front of her, and I lunged for it, just barely missing. She took a few steps back and my mother, still laughing, lunged forward. Any hesitation dissolved rather quickly, and we all three crawled forward as Sara made the red ball of feathers dance around the room. Sensations heightened as we crawled around on the floor and yet, surprisingly, my knees never hurt, my arms never ached, my focus remained acutely attuned to the moment. I felt my tail, I don't know how exactly, sway in balance with the movement of my crawling. The catsuit was an easy second skin, and we fell into the charade with renewed effort and frenzy. Ravioli, his interest piqued, jumped up and followed, rolling into us and swatting at our fur.

We followed Sara into the dining room. My dad climbed up onto the table, sat for a moment on his haunches, and swatted again at the ball of red feathers. We crawled through the den, sniffed under furniture, scooted around on the carpet. Ravioli approached me, rolled onto his belly, then back to all fours. It was the most active I'd seen him for some time. In the kitchen, my mother sat by the glass back door gazing for a moment at squirrels.

"Keep it up," said Sarah. "Ravioli is really engaging now."

We rounded the corner to the long hallway. Sara dipped into my parents' room, which was closest to the den. We crawled in mewing and yawing. My mother swatted a bottle of melatonin off my father's side table. I rolled around on the bed until my mother came and stretched out on top of me. Her body was warm and heavy, it made the suit scratch even more but she seemed to be enjoying herself, and I let her claw with abandon. My father sat at the end of the bed, swiping at the bedspread while Ravioli extended his front paws and chipped away at the bedpost.

In my room, my father began knocking things off my desk: swatting pens, paper, and a stapler onto the floor, creating a mess.

"Hey," I said, through my mask. Sara swatted my haunches with the toy. From nowhere she produced a small spray bottle and squirted water in my face. The droplets came through the mask's eyeholes and, not being able to wipe them away, I groaned and rubbed my face into the carpet. Ravioli slunk up in apparent solidarity and rubbed his nose next to mine. The cat versions of my mother and father sidled up to us with a roiling energy, and we spilled back into the hallway.

Sara jiggled the ball of feathers farther away, pausing for a moment before opening Jacob's door and disappearing into his room. My father and I turned our cat faces to my mother. She started forward then stopped to smooth her whiskers with the back of her paw. Ravioli crept slowly up to the door's frame but didn't go inside.

The red ball of feathers landed in Jacob's doorway, and I swatted before Sara jerked it back into the darkness of the room. Once I had crawled inside, she threw the toy over my head and out into the hallway once more, where my mother and father lingered. My mom moved one black paw, then another toward the doorway, and I watched as my father's orange fur crawled behind her with trepidation. My mother mewed, and my father purred next to her as they made their way into Jacob's room together. Ravioli peeked his head around the corner, then stretched out into the room, clawing at the carpet.

It was clear by now the suits amplified smell, because the room still had Jacob's odor. Even months after he was gone, notes of chemical sourness from his body sprays wafted through my cat mask. The carpet was pushed down with the musk of his muddy sneakers. Old gym clothes, pungent with dried sweat, still gathered in a bin in the corner. We crawled around breathing in reminders of his body's mark on the world, and while it was mystifying to feel Jacob so present and immediate, the heightened state made me more intently aware of how truly gone he was.

Ravioli darted around the room, and we crawled behind him as he slid his body along Jacob's dresser, then bed frame, then desk. My mother used her claws to pull a dirty shirt from Jacob's hamper, and she rolled around with it on the floor. My father spotted an old grapefruit peel on Jacob's desk, knocked it off and swatted at it like a soccer ball. Ravioli followed, pushing the peel under the bed then back out the other side, where he lunged at my tail as if to play. Sara stepped over us to stand in the corner and observe.

My mother disengaged her claws from the dirty shirt and climbed onto Jacob's bed, digging a small space in the blankets to lie down. My dad jumped up behind her, leaned his back close to her cat body, and wrapped a clawed paw around her black fur. Ravioli and I followed, and my parents folded their legs enough for us all to curl up in the center of the bed. We inched into each other, forming a giant ball of heat and fur, purring and slowing our breathing until we fell asleep, exhausted by the intensity of the new world around us.

I'm not sure how much time passed, but my mother began to stir and turned to take off her mask. She was half-under my leg, my father's arm lying atop her face. My father stirred and took his mask off, his feet still curled around my stomach. My mother stood and hung her suit over her arm like a towel. When I sat up and removed my mask, my father rubbed me behind my actual ears, and adjusted Ravioli who had moved to his lap. We folded our suits and made our way back to the living room. Sara was gone, the tracks of her pink suitcase led from the center of the living room to the front door. She left a business card on the table.

* * *

I left for college less than a month later, graduated down the line with a degree in social work, years later with a master's, then doctorate, in psychoanalysis. Ravioli lived a few more years and died from old age, wrapped up on the love seat in one of Jacob's shirts while my mother, father, and I sang to him from inside the suits we still had.

The cats continued to jump all throughout my college years. It spread exponentially across the world until no corner of the earth was left untouched. More and more cats in Africa, Asia, and isolated islands of New Zealand offed themselves in tremendously horrific jumps. They fell in Switzerland, Russia, remote areas of mountainous China, sand-strewn islands, and tree-rich forests across the globe. They landed on bricks and chewing-gum wrappers with the same resounding thuds until the upsetting behavior was finally linked back to a recessive gene triggered by poor diet and social determinants—such as the cumulative stress of cats having to shoulder the sadness of humans on a daily basis. In the end, it was only four percent of the cat population, but the discovery made us pause for a year or so. We examined ourselves as a people, confronted some demons we all would have rather kept swept under our collective rugs. There were some international committees and tribunals, some protestors who marched for a time through streets cordoned off by aluminum railings, some peer-reviewed journals that relegated feline research to footnotes in science journals read only by scientists. By the time I earned my certification, the world was back to normal. A pill crushed daily into wet food seemed to keep our cats happy and healthy, and we medicated them out of our own selfishness to ensure that they would stay alive with us. Comfort us. Help us get out of bed in the morning, open doors, live.

TRAVIS EISENBISE *holds an MFA in Creative Writing from the University of North Carolina at Greensboro, and his fiction has appeared in* Joyland *and* Denver Quarterly. *He lives in Brooklyn, New York and is allergic to cats.*

Something to Do With Time

Eliza Robertson

The Masters Review Vol. V, "Pirates of Penance," selected by Amy Hempel

For many years, I was the writer who strove for a novel and wound up with 5,000 words. If I didn't aspire to write a novel? I'd be lucky to get 3,500. And while I admired the architectural brilliance required of a well-laid novel, I was someone who hotly declared short stories the superior form. So it's with some disquiet that I admit I haven't written a story in two years. Not because I don't adore the genre. Not because I find long-form prose easier. Not because I let commercial pressures *totally* dictate the projects I embark on. I suppose it has something to do with time.

In 2015, I stumbled on a real-life event that haunted me until I worked it into a book-length manuscript. I'm nearing the finish line of that work now, and between my day jobs and side gigs, I haven't had much room in my days to write stories. When *The Masters Review* contacted me to write this essay, I read over the story that had appeared in their Volume V anthology, edited by Amy Hempel back in 2016. It was the first time I'd read one of my own stories in years, and my infatuation with the genre came flooding back to me.

The seeds of my stories vary. Sometimes it's an image or a place that wriggles into my imagination. Sometimes it's a line—the sway of the first words as they find me, which I milk until I run out of fuel. However, the *Masters Review* story, "Pirates of Penance," was rooted in an emotion that isn't flattering or easy to admit. I wrote that story because I was jealous. I wanted to write about jealousy, and especially the jealousy that can attend feminine competition.

What few writers discuss in the open is their envy—that particular tang we feel when another person gets published, or wins an award. I think we should talk about our jealousies more openly in the hopes of defanging them. I have entire text threads with close writer friends that chronicle the ego bruises of another writer's success. What I appreciate about these text threads is their absurdity—and thank God, because we need some humor to rustle us out of our self-absorbed habits of comparison.

There's writer envy, and there's admiration—reserved for folks who are far enough beyond our current stations that we see them as icons or mentors. I had long admired Amy Hempel's writing, as I had the other femme authors of salty tragicomic prose (such as Lorrie Moore, Lydia Davis, Mary Robison). In the fiction workshops I taught at the University of East Anglia or the UK's National Centre for Writing, I always taught a Hempel story. Thus it was with glee and disbelief that she selected my story as a winner in the 2016 competition.

Some people are evolved enough to feel that same admiration—rather than envy—for their peers. I am not so evolved, and I feel compassion toward any other writer who experiences a stab of cortisol every time someone else wins or reaches a milestone they themselves have been toiling after.

And yet: comparison is futile. You're guaranteed to write your worst work if you silo yourself into a chamber of writing to please judges, or publishers, or MFA instructors, or coursemates. At the best of times, jealousy can fuel inspiration, and my advice is to pump that silver lining for all it's worth.

There's a line in "Pirates of Penance"—*I had been feeling cruel since Art left—wishing small ills upon others, pleased when a raging child in Hyde Park got splattered with seagull shit.* What started as a neti pot for whatever envy was congesting my mind at the time turned into a story about refusing the separateness that jealousy can instill. It's about making friends of rivals and witnessing the folly of our own habits of comparison, or assuming the grass is always greener.

If there's one piece of advice I find important to share, it's to feel compassion for the side of you that still looks over the fence. At the same time, get curious about how to metamorphose that venom into genuine friendship, camaraderie, or fuel.

ELIZA ROBERTSON's *2014 debut collection,* Wallflowers, *was shortlisted for the East Anglia Book Award, the Danuta Gleed Short Story Prize, and selected as a* New York Times Editor's Choice. *Her critically acclaimed first novel,* Demi-Gods, *was a* Globe & Mail *and* National Post *book of the year and the winner of the 2018 QWF Paragraphe Hugh MacLennan Prize. She studied creative writing at the University of Victoria and the University of East Anglia, where she received the Man Booker Scholarship and Curtis Brown Prize. In addition to being shortlisted for the CBC Short Story Prize and Journey Prize, Eliza's stories have won the Commonwealth Short Story Prize, 2017 Elizabeth Jolley Prize, and 2019 3Macs carte blanche Prize. Originally from Vancouver Island, Eliza lives in Montreal.*

Persimmon

Elissa C. Huang

Ling-Si just caught the last evening bus out of the depot, bones heavy, clothes wet, the metal spokes of his umbrella distended, the fabric floppy and torn. His face was round and pitted, a wretched brown moon. Fumbling in his pockets, he fished out the coins needed to make the passage up to Queens. As the metal clattered into the fare box, the driver shut the door behind him and lurched through the tunnel, not bothering to wait. Everyone was tired, wanting to get home and get dry. Ling-Si surveyed the bus for an empty seat. Many of the younger riders had their ears muffled in headphones, their faces lit up by screens, oblivious to the elder in front of them who wasn't yet too feeble to stand. Ling-Si hooked his elbow around a pole, letting his legs sway loosely with every hard turn. The straps of the plastic bag cut into his palm, the round fruits inside straining to break loose.

The air on the bus stank of bitter coffee and damp leather. It had been another long day and he longed to get back to warmth and his girlfriend, to nuzzle the baby's neck, the soft folds of her skin warm and sticky with mother's milk, her silky tufts of hair catching in his stubble. As the bus jerked to a halt, the riders pushed forward single file the same way they shoved on in the mornings, a desperate rush against time. A woman thundered down the stairs, her purse snagging on Ling-Si's bag, tearing it open. She pounded on the back door to *Open the fuck up*, not bothering to look back as his persimmons—now free of their plastic prison—rolled in every direction, their waxy orange skins bright against the dark ridges on the floor. He scrambled for them on his hands and knees. People lightly kicked the strays in his direction, others bent over and handed them to him. Grateful for the help, he clutched the fruit to his chest.

He quickly dropped into an open seat, unzipped his jacket at the neck, and deposited the salvaged fruit into his makeshift pouch. They were cold and hard, pressing against the warmth of his belly. With a sigh, he let the tension drop from his shoulders momentarily. In his dreams, he rode an infinite loop of identical roadways jammed with headlights and blaring horns, never arriving at his destination. Trying not to nod off, the parade of raindrops was a sheet of hypnotic ancestral sound, beckoning him to give in to the exhaustion. *Close your eyes, my son,* they seemed to say. *Follow us into the dark.*

* * *

The boss yanked the fabric out of one of the women's machines, breaking the needle. As she yelled at the woman that the seams were uneven, nobody said a word. Ling-Si made the mistake of pausing from his mundane task of hanging the garments and she turned her wrath onto him instead. "You there! Something interesting for you to look at?" she snarled. He shook his head no. She never bothered with learning their names. Their bodies were disposable, their names of even less consequence. *I have a name,* he quietly raged. It was a name his parents had prayed on, dreamed of, and reflected upon before bestowing it upon him, their only child. A formidable lineage of farmers and warriors, teachers and poets, people who worked with their hands and minds, all gone now. So far as he knew, his family was the last of his bloodline. His wife and children back in China had been counting on him; the rest of their relations had vanished, lost to tragedies born from political exodus. But he could not bear for them to see him like this: his two weathered arms, thick with veins and scars, in this dingy downtown sweatshop, just another faceless worker. After the first year had passed, they stopped waiting for him to send for them.

Nobody knew when the sun rose or set in that concrete room. They were only allowed to get up to relieve themselves during timed breaks. There were buckets to piss into when the toilets overflowed as they often did, and in the summer, the stench grew unbearable with the sour sweat emanating from their drenched clothes, threadbare compared to the luxurious silks they stitched and mined out to the city's fashion houses and department stores. In the winter, their fingers moved slower, stiff from the cold. But the pay was often better than in the restaurants, and most of them were like him, refugees indebted to the local Chinatown gangs who kept them safe from discovery.

One of the men spit blood into the sink. He had a tooth that required an extraction, but he would need to let it rot out. The workers didn't speak to one another much, though their disparate dialects may have been similar enough. The men and women ate together, but slept apart in unregistered buildings not up to code, crammed to the hilt with rows of aluminum-frame bunk beds. They were intimate strangers. Some sobbed quietly into their pillows at night from the loneliness, trying to muffle their ragged breaths; others disappeared without a trace only to be replaced with another the next day. Mostly, they stayed silent because to speak would have given voice to the questions: *Is this all that I am? Is this all I'll ever be?*

* * *

"Did you get them?" she asked. Her face was sharp with sunken, dark hollows for eyes. When he first met her, her cheeks had been plump, her lips full and pink.

He nodded.

"Did you get them from the stall in Rooster Alley?"

He nodded again.

A single bare bulb hung in the center of the dark room, like a soft beam of interrogation. He gently laid the fruits on the table, one at a time. In the dim light, they glowed and pulsed with life.

As he sat on the stool, he inhaled sharply, trying not to wince.

She yanked up his sleeve roughly. A makeshift bandage had been wrapped around his inner elbow, now darkened with crusted blood.

"How much did they take this time?"

"It doesn't matter."

"Tell me."

"More than the last."

Her face softened then, her eyes beckoned to him, her mouth dripped with words both cajoling and sweet. Chun-Yu was young, young enough to be his daughter. When he first tried to lay with her, she had mocked him for staring too long at her swelled belly, four months with child. *Never mind,* she had said. *That's nothing to do with you.* He remembered his youngest, an infinite ocean away, not yet able to walk when he left. When Chun-Yu tried to reach for Ling-Si, he pulled away sharply, shaking his head, his mind swirling with regret. He was so pitiful, she couldn't bring herself to kick him out.

When the baby arrived, a little girl with thunderous screams, he stopped Chun-Yu from doing an awful thing; the cries drove her to madness. He'd tell her to sleep, rocking the baby for hours, atoning for lost time. Once Chun-Yu returned to herself, she was able to love her daughter with an all-consuming ferocity. He came by once a week at first, then more often as they grew dependent on each other for company.

Li-Sing found the cutting board. Chun-Yu's eyes glistened with hunger as he carefully peeled and cut the fruit, juice running across his fingers and down his forearms, sticky and sweet. He slid a plate over to her. Her mouth, a cavern of gnashing teeth, consumed the persimmons as if they were air and water, sun and life. *Careful,* he warned her. *Take it easy.* But she paid him no mind and soon she was lost, her eyes glazed into bliss. He watched enviously as she slipped away.

As Ling-Si took his first bite, letting the flesh and pulp slide down his throat, he was transported home. His wife, a foggy outline behind a curtain of steam, was in the next room, so close he could almost touch her again. A pot of stew was on the stove, the grassy scent of herbs swirling through the air. He couldn't remember her face. *Why?* He took another bite, and all became sharper. *The kids. If he could only see his son again. If he could only lift his daughter up into the air one more time.* His heart ached to get closer. Her hair was black and dull, knotted tightly at the nape of her neck, her dress a faded cornflower blue. Her hands were tiny and moving, constantly busy. Hummingbird wings. Reaching for one of them, he tried to capture it in his own, to still her momentarily, but the apparition vanished. Too soon, too soon again he was back in Chun-Yu's empty and cold kitchen. They had devoured all the fruit. He blinked until his focus came back and found her licking the paring knife, a slight trace of blood tinging her lips.

"Enough." His voice was kind as he gently wrestled the knife out of her hands. She didn't put up much of a fight, drifting into the bedroom, leaving her door ajar. It was left open for the men who would come later in the evening. Like Ling-Si, she was trapped in purgatory, never able to leave, never able to go home due to the shame. She was stuck with the men who had brought her here, the men who used her body, the men who gave and took her money. And now, the man who gave her an escape, however momentary.

Time passed like molasses except for when they were together in this persimmon haze. And then it was jagged and slashed at their hearts until reality was memory, memory was fantasy, until all was gone. As the earth turned its way into dawn, the sun peered over the horizon in a streak of peach fire stretching from end to end. Ling-Si remembered his first bite, thinking he had been poisoned. A thought so ridiculous now that he couldn't fathom a day without it. He left behind his slumbering wards and rode the bus back to begin another day.

* * *

Rooster Alley was so named because of how early the vendors set up before the rest of the market. By dawn, most of what they sold was gone. They only took payment in gold or blood. Sometimes a wealthy patron would slip out from the shadows, trying not to be seen among the depraved. Truth is, they all had the sickness, regardless of whether they wore silks or rags.

"Look who's back again."

"Please," he began, rolling his sleeve up.

The tiny old woman looked at his arm with disdain. "You've nothing left to give me. Go home."

A small crate of persimmons sat there, the fruit huddled tightly against each other, shivering in the cold, as if they were beckoning for him to rescue them. They were redder, with thin veins of gold juice glimmering underneath their skins. He had never seen this kind before and he became possessed by the thought, *I must have one.*

"What are those?"

"Those are not for you."

Li-Sing's pupils went dark and he lunged at her with a force that surprised him; he shoved the fruit into his mouth and managed to take a ravenous bite before being swiftly subdued by her two sons. They twisted his arms behind his back and shoved him to the ground, kicking his ribs over and over as he curled into himself.

"Pity," he sputtered, begging. "Take pity!"

They beat him until he was a pile of pulpy flesh, blood and spit dribbling out of his mouth. Over and over they hit him with blind fury, wanting to break him into a thousand pieces, until the life had left his body. He bit his tongue and blacked out from the pain, the last sound in his ears a woman's scream, perhaps his wife's from across the sea. When he came to, it was high noon and the alley was empty, like a phantom mirage.

He could not move, could only see a sliver of the street through his rapidly swelling eyes, the sidewalk rough and cold on his cheek, something warm and wet spilling out from him, pooling around him, lifting him up into the air. Grunting with effort, he moved to press his mangled hand to his face, to see if he was really still there. His palm was sticky with persimmon juice and he forced himself to chew the stolen bite pocketed in his cheek. The persimmon had smashed beneath his torso and was now flattened a few feet away from him, just out of reach. Undeterred, he clawed his way slowly to it, dragging his broken leg behind him.

At last, he made it. His chest was aching, the beginning of a death rattle forcing out his last breaths. Ling-Si pried his lips open, stretching his tongue out to suck up and lap at the orange stain of the fruit, the last of its meat. His eyes closed completely, denying his tears escape. Fractured visions danced across the insides of his lids like a kaleidoscope: Chun-Yu leaning over the sink, a glass horn cupped against her breast as she squeezes the rubber bulb to pull the golden milk out of her body. Ling-Si cuts the fruit into tiny pieces for the baby, mashing it up with his fingers, thinning it out with the milk. The baby sucks the fruit mash from Ling-Si's fingers, her tiny lips flayed out, suckling with urgency.

Atop a mountain at midday, his wife at his side, no more words between them. The sky bright and clear, the air fresh and crisp with cypress. Behind him, his son hides in the house, too angry to come out and wish him safe travels. His infant daughter, sleeping and unaware. He leaves them all, walks down the narrow dirt path into the valley. The train ride is long and bumpy. The flight across the ocean, longer. His insides shake with fear and panic at the hubbub upon landing, a din of metropolitan noise that overwhelms his senses.

Months later, he cuts the baby bigger pieces of persimmon so she can gnaw on it with her gums. Her bliss gives him comfort.

His wife stops writing. Mercifully, she stops asking questions of him that he cannot answer. A lock of hair is enclosed in her last letter, the thin paper crinkled and the ink splotched. He presses it to his face, inhales, trying to remember the smoothness of her cheek, his fingers lost in the coarseness of her thick hair.

Later now, maybe years later, he is still cutting fruit after every meal, sticking little toothpicks in each bite. Chun-Yu speaks less and less. Her daughter, when she finds language and words, sits and talks with him instead. They make up stories into the night.

He continues to send money to the village every month, hoping that it will be received, hoping that his children do not think of him with too much hatred.

And a few more years pass, time always so sudden. Chun-Yu's daughter grows sullen, clings to her mother, afraid of him and the other men in her life. He sees that she has changed and he is stricken helpless, unable to stop it. He continues to cut the fruit, a peace offering, but it doesn't stop the anger in the house. Mother and daughter fight, words are shouted. Old enough now, her daughter moves out.

His letters come back, unopened. One is marked with the characters for "Deceased" hastily scribbled in black pen on the envelope. After, he drinks too much whiskey, wakes up on a park bench in a light drizzle, his pockets emptied.

Days in the sweatshop continue until they lock him out, tell him to go elsewhere. Time moves even quicker now and his body can no longer keep pace. Maybe he notices that Chun-Yu is beautiful. Maybe when she turns, she is faceless, too. Eventually, he forgets what she looks like, is unable to recall the shape of her eyes, the slope of her nose and chin. Soon, he forgets his face in youth; he's used to the old man that stares back at him in the mirror.

He sees that her body has begun to stoop, that she has begun to limp. She makes a small comment about an ache in her hip. She attempts to make an herbal salve, but drops the contents of the medicinal pouch. The dark powder hits the floor, a dust cloud. He urges her to sit, reaches for the mortar and pestle.

Not too much later, weeks that feel like minutes, Chun-Yu succumbs to the sickness and leaves him all alone. Her daughter shows up in time for the funeral, a simple Buddhist service, and they sit in silence until she gets up to cut the fruit. She offers him some. Maybe he has lost his teeth, maybe the fruit is too hard, maybe she will slip and cut her finger and it bleeds so badly, they almost need to take her to the hospital. And maybe, wordlessly, he gets up and does it for her, this one small task he can still manage though his hands shake slightly.

And as he cuts, warm tears run down the deep creases on his face, splashing on the counter. They eat the salty fruit, a small release of pain. Minutes pass like seconds.

Now he floats, higher and higher, out of the room, past Chun-Yu's photo over the altar, out of the dingy hallway, onto the dirty street, through the city still asleep but slowly waking, drunks sprawled out on the sidewalks and in the parks, a young couple fighting, the man yelling louder, berating the woman, past the gold chains on the red velvet pillows in shop windows, the people flipping their signs from open to closed, from closed to open. A shopkeeper sets out a display of plastic toys: yapping dogs running on batteries, turning flips, running into the edge, going nowhere. Tiny jars of tiny swimming turtles, rows and rows of baked pastries on trays, bowl after bowl of steaming rice porridge and sweet soy milk. A storm is coming, the sky flat and gray. He hears the sound of the thunder rolling, or maybe it's just the creak from a storefront steel gate unlocking, hard and angry.

All this he will see and think, *Maybe this was a good life. I am real, this is real.*

He sees his body sprawled out on the ground, wills himself to sit up. Her "Where were you?" goes unanswered. One look, one gasp at his bloodied face, and she ushers him inside quickly, even though he is empty handed but for the toy dog barking in his hand. It does not stop.

ELISSA C. HUANG *received her MFA in Dramatic Writing from NYU's Tisch School of the Arts. She has won the John Golden Playwriting Prize and the Goldberg Prize in Playwriting.*

Her plays, "Bruce & Lee" and "Arctic Circle" (as the "e" in e.b. lee) are published by Playscripts; her play "8 Minutes Left" (again, as the "e" in e.b. lee) is published by Stage Partners. She was the fiction winner of the 2019 Iron Horse Literary Review's Trifecta Competition *and her fiction has appeared in* Sycamore Review, Iron Horse Literary Review, Hyphen Magazine, *and* Cheat River Review.

Never Stop Learning, and Other Things I Learned Along the Way

Emma Sloley

The Masters Review Vol. VII, "The Sand Nests," selected by Rebecca Makkai

One sultry evening in 2018 I sat on a curb outside a bookstore and listened to Rachel Kushner read from one of her novels to a rapt crowd that spilled out into the street. I had spent most of that summer in Paris, lurking around Shakespeare and Company and wondering when I was going to feel like a real writer. (Extremely Lost Generation of me, I know.) I had only been writing fiction in a serious way for three years, which is about a microsecond in writer years, and I was suffering from all the usual self-doubt. I had no MFA, no connections, and no real idea what I was doing, beyond a kind of floundering instinctual understanding of what made a story alive. I had been writing for fashion and travel magazines for years, but I was shocked at how little my time at the journalism coalface had prepared me for the transition into fiction. I felt like I was starting again, word by painful word, endeavoring to reach a place where my sentences did what I wanted them to.

There's no bad time to get good news. But it felt especially charmed that a message arrived at that moment of mopey doubt letting me know my short story "The Sand Nests" had been chosen for the next *Masters Review* anthology. Had I arrived? Well, maybe not a Rachel Kushner-level of arrival, but it felt like I had passed through some magical portal into the world where the other writers hung out, the ones whose books I admired and whose careers I longed to emulate. Writers like Rebecca Makkai, who chose my story along with the other brilliant talents who appeared in the anthology that year. Rebecca was so kind and encouraging, she provided a blueprint for the kind of writer I wanted to be, not just on the page but in my dealings with others in the publishing world.

Since that summer, I've published my first novel and had many more short stories appear in dream journals, but I haven't forgotten and will likely never forget the thrill of that anthology acceptance, and what it meant to have my work affirmed in that way at such a crucial moment in my career. A few things I learned along the way:

> **Never stop learning.** I still feel like a beginner in so many ways, and I don't mean that self-deprecatingly. It's exciting to feel like you still have so much to learn. I make it part of my writing routine to read about craft, listen to other short story writers and novelists talk about their work through bookstore readings, literary events, and podcasts, and to follow brilliant writers on social media. I also recommend applying for residencies and writing conferences (particularly fully funded ones or those that offer scholarships), joining writing groups, and reading for literary magazines.
>
> **Know when to start the story.** One of the magazine editors I knew in my early career was always gently pointing out

that I had started the story in the wrong place. "Here," they would tap with their red pen at a point several paragraphs down from where I'd started, "here's your lede." Inevitably, they were right. Like many writers, my opening lines are often full of throat-clearing, unnecessary detail that bogs the story down. Relatedly, multiple beginnings. This can be a problem of enthusiasm. Every path of the story is so fascinating that it's impossible to choose one, so it's tempting to try to go down all the paths at once.

Develop your voice. That thing you're obsessed with? Those motifs you keep returning to? The weird and singular way in which you express what it's like to be human and striving in the world? Those are all parts of your aesthetic, your unique voice, and the best thing you can do for your writing is cultivate that weirdness and make it so that something you've written could only have been written by you.

Be the kind of writer you needed when you were starting out. You never forget the people who offered you kindness, support, and guidance when you were emerging, and the emerging writers you offer the same will never forget you either.

***EMMA SLOLEY**'s work has appeared in* Catapult, Literary Hub, Yemassee, Joyland, *and* The Common, *among many others. She is a MacDowell fellow and a Bread Loaf scholar, and her debut novel,* DISASTER'S CHILDREN, *was published by Little A books in 2019. Born in Australia, Emma now divides her time between the US and the city of Mérida, Mexico.*

The Bird Rattle

Chelsy Diaz Amaya

I am not my grandmother's carbon copy, but I believe we've always had the same number of eyelashes. Days after she passes, my mother shows me a picture of her and says we both have "so much face." I put my finger on her cheek, trace up to her nose, and back to her cheek. In bed, before sleep, I often close my eyes and take her picture, place it into a shoebox, upside down. I want to give her something else to look at. I throw the shoebox in the ocean. It floats farther and farther away.

* * *

Moments before she died, Mom asked her for *la bendición* and my grandmother spoke: *en el nombre del padre, del hijo, y del espiritu santo.* And then my mother handed the phone to me and there was a pause, a brief thirteen-second pause. I know because I was holding my breath as I counted and then she made a sound. Weekends became dim and I was stuck on my grandmother's death rattle while my mother became more bone than woman, forgetting to eat, forgetting to talk, forgetting to get out of bed. An echo of the Alzheimer's my grandmother had.

* * *

I recognize the heavy breathing, the gargling phlegm. In the months after my grandmother dies, I am excessively preoccupied with searching for evidence. I want to know that what I heard was real. I watch spirit orbs ascend, little circular dashes of light, and I wonder if her orb has made it to heaven yet. I feel this is wrong. I am intruding in a stranger's last and most vulnerable moment but these strangers sound like each other and none of them sound like her.

"This isn't right," I tell Mom, exasperated.

She responds with tired eyes, "There isn't a wrong way to die."

I read articles listed under the search: "death rattle." I find three treatments to minimize the noise: reposition the body, limit fluid intake, and mouth care, but I do not want treatment. I want translation.

"Maybe she was blowing you a kiss," Mom says. The smacking of her moth-thin lips, is that what's haunting me? I read a book of Ecuadorian myths and songs by Amazonian Quichuas, known as the Napo Runa, who associate women with birds. Women transform into hummingbirds and ducks. In one song, a woman transforms into a hummingbird and calls herself a cloud woman.

I pursue the sound until every early morning, when I open my bedroom blinds, I see hummingbirds. They make my heart beat so fast it feels like I'm going through life backward. I see my grandmother in them, as if she's shapeshifted.

In my dreams, I no longer place the picture in the shoebox. Instead, I am with her. Stuck. I try waking up, moving, turning, twitching my fingers, but my body is lifeless, my mind awake. There must be a stillness in her empty house, the lonely land.

* * *

In my book of myths, I read about Santo Domingo de los Tsáchilas, known as *el pueblo de los colorados* because natives there are known for coloring their hair with achiote seeds. When *el Tigre de la Oscuridad* or the Tiger of Darkness ate the sun because he was ravenous, there was endless night and no reflection in this city. Hopeful, the shamans prepared ayahuasca for a young man. After drinking what the shamans provided, the young man began to cry luminous tears as his body slowly began to elevate. He became the sun. This is rumored to have occurred *hace muchisimos años atras, cuando los abuelos podian conversar con los pájaros* or many years ago, when grandparents could speak with birds.

* * *

Let me start again. She had Alzheimer's and I never met her and she forgot me first. She died across an ocean. I was in the Mohawk Valley and she was in the Andes Mountains, but I was the one who heard her death rattle. It was not a choking sound. It sounded like chirping. It was chirping. Like a baby bird.

* * *

I met Aunt Ruth a year after my grandmother passed away. She flew to New York to visit us. All I knew about her was that she was the only aunt of mine who could not have children. Upon seeing her my first thought was, "She looks nothing like Mom," but I did not tell my mother this until after she left. Aunt Ruth has different eyes, nose, lips, and coloring to her skin. She moves and talks differently. She looks most like my grandmother, more than any of my other aunts and uncles. "Everyone else seems to look more like your grandfather," my mother said, offering an explanation.

* * *

On a hot June night, Aunt Ruth's husband, Rodrigo, and my father were on the patio chatting. He had come to visit us in New York some time before Aunt Ruth visited. He was pouring me beer whenever my dad's head was turned. When my father decided he was too tired to stick around, he told me to turn off the garage lights and go to bed, too. When I was a couple of steps from entering the back door, Rodrigo asked me to help him dial a number on his phone, claiming he still hadn't learned how to use it.

As I was dialing it for him, I felt his arm constrict around my waist. He pulled me closer to his body. I had tried getting up or maybe I was drunk and thought I tried, but he would not let me go. He told me to finish dialing. When I passed the phone back, his arm was still around me. It was so quiet, every ring sounded like a prayer. When we saw the kitchen light turn on, his arm loosened, and I walked inside so quickly, I left my flip-flops outside. I did not go near him for the rest of his visit. I stopped calling him "uncle."

The next morning, I told my mother about Rodrigo grabbing me. I must not have presented it as an issue because all she said was that he used to do that to her when she was a teen, too. She told me he had had an affair with one of her cousins when she was very young. This cousin became pregnant and left for Spain.

"She's never been back to Sevilla," Mom said. "Sometimes, I think we made it all up."

* * *

It's over three years since she's passed when my connecting flight from Dallas to Quito turns around midflight due to a volcanic eruption in the Eastern Andes. I sleep on the Dallas carpet dust. I have no mouthwash and my hair is greasy.

On the second plane to Quito, a flight attendant tells me I am green. My body senses the altitude. The pilot announces he must fly us in circles because the plane still has too much fuel to land safely. Once I feel the first turn, it takes everything in me not to vomit on the man to my right. Everyone else reads, watches movies, or sleeps, and I panic because no one else is. I think of the *cuvivíes* or plover birds, who migrate from the north of the United States to the lagoons of Ozogoche. They are known as *el ave suicidio* and there is still no clear scientific or mythological explanation as to why these birds, upon arriving to Ecuador's lagoons, plummet into the freezing waters and die.

For thousands of years, the Quichua, Ecuador's most populous Indigenous group, have treated their suicide as sacred. They collect the dead birds for food and hold a yearly festival. Many scientists have dismissed the claim that the birds commit any kind of suicide. I remember reading that the *cuvivíes* have to be severely affected by the change in air pressure, that the length of their journey causes a disorientation so severe, it results in thermal shock. When the plane jerks to a stop and *el chulla quiteño* plays through the speakers, we erupt into applause and I am the first to clap.

* * *

Aunt Ruth and her husband Rodrigo come to Quito to pick me up and take me back with them to Sevilla de Oro, my mother's hometown, a small parish reliant on agriculture and a hydroelectric power plant. The ten-hour drive from Quito to Sevilla de Oro nearly kills me. At first, I didn't know it would take ten hours, and after four, I ask if we're near. *Don't even think about Sevilla yet,* they laugh. Other than the dizziness, what I remember most from the Pan-American Highway is a little girl I saw herding sheep at the tip of a tall mountain.

That night, I am sick, violently sick. I press my hot clammy cheek against the bathroom floor. Behind my eyelids, I see the outline of my grandmother's body sitting on a rocking chair as she knits outside of her wooden home. "What's happening to me?" I ask aloud in the quiet calm of the bathroom, my voice echoing. I am cold and sweaty and dehydrated. I can't help but think that the difficulty of my journey to Sevilla de Oro is a form of punishment. A disorientation so severe. I fall asleep on the floor. In a dream, I see my grandmother unfazed and distant. Sitting on her chair, she lowers her eyes to me and says, "I've been stuck here waiting. What took you so long?"

* * *

Aunt Ruth and Rodrigo live next to my grandmother's land. My mother has told me that the land on which they built their house was Ruth's inheritance, so none of the remaining land corresponds to them, but this was a verbal agreement between them and my grandmother, and no written record exists. Since the owner of the property is deceased, the town has threatened to take the land away, but to avoid arguments between each other, my aunts and uncles have still not made any decision about how to divide it. Rodrigo still wants more land, wants the strip of land closest to them, says there will be more room for his chickens. Maybe a cow. For now, the only time the land welcomes life is during the yearly family reunion organized by my cousins. Otherwise, the land is desolate.

* * *

When I am feeling better, I walk around Sevilla de Oro and stop at my grandmother's house before walking down the block to Aunt Ruth's. I like looking at the picture of Jesus my grandmother framed in thin silver on her front porch. I want to touch the gold plaque of the family's name above the door. If I stacked a pile of cement blocks to touch it, it would still be too high to reach. Every time I get the urge to touch the plaque, I remember how the first time I visited my grandmother's tombstone, all I wanted was to feel the cold wood of her coffin.

In Sevilla de Oro, people have stopped me to ask, *Usted es hija de quien?* or *You're the daughter of whom?* Their eyes have widened when I have boldly responded with her name.

The daughter of Victoria Berzosa and Antonio Amaya, who left Sevilla to find work. Then, returned with a husband and announced she was leaving for America in three days.

My mother, the myth.

Strangers have turned out to be cousins. Women have claimed they visited my grandmother every day when she was ill, have cooked her dinner, have fed her animals. They have told me how brave, and strong, and wise she was.

My grandmother, the past.

When I told one of these strangers I was staying with my Aunt Ruth, I received disapproval. A much older man wearing a dark-blue heavy poncho, holding a bottle of whiskey, had grunted and it startled me.

"*Tía*," he had repeated and shook his head, disappointed. His face was so wrinkled I could barely look him in the eye.

My aunt, the mystery.

Except for a lone cow grazing the field, the land is still. I think of all the stories I have been told, all of them affected by time and memory, and how over the passage of time, I'll have more stories to add. I imagine, once the grass was tall. My mother and her siblings, my mother's mother and her siblings, running through it. I want this house to speak, to sit with me and start from the beginning, to etch my family's truth into its glass windows, to transform its cracked cement into calligraphy. The cow lies on its side and gives birth. Feet first, then nose. After some time, the calf walks alongside its mother, crooked steps turning graceful, time passing them, too.

* * *

I also read about a young man, known as the Huacay Siqui, from the province of Pichincha, who had a mother who was very ill. He took care of her every night, but on one occasion, he left her bedside because he needed to buy her medicine. He ran into his lover and she invited him to a dance. He accepted, forgetting his sick mother. While they were dancing, he felt he was falling deeper in love and when other men interrupted them to inform him of his mother's death, he responded, "There will be time to cry."

When Tupá, the supreme God, saw how little he valued his mother, he decided to punish him by transforming him into a bird that cries at night. The birds leave their ravine at night and sing a gloomy song that sounds like a human cry. They cause people accidents and when they fly near homes where a baby's clothes are drying outside, the bird will peck at the clothes and the baby will begin to cry.

* * *

"*Buenos días, Doña Ruth, me puede dar unas hierbitas de ataco?*" A little girl's voice, asking for some ataco leaves, which are used to calm the soul. I peek over the fence and notice sun-streaked tears, a chapped bottom lip jutting outwardly. I turn to my aunt, who asks the girl to follow her to the other side of her garden. My aunt's deft fingers pick and separate seeds and leaves. She puts the worthy ones in a small pot until it's full. She mothers the little girl. She plays with her hair, speaks to her calmly, offers her a meal.

"*Quien murió?*" I ask. The girl ignores me. My aunt gives me a pointed look. I've made the girl uncomfortable by asking who died, but ataco leaves are given to those grieving, those in excessive shock or pain. The girl hugs my aunt and walks out of the garden, perfectly white tennis shoes a sharp contrast to her black clothes.

Aunt Ruth has always wanted children. She's told me stories about the many in vitro fertilization procedures, how the doctors took her eggs, the discomfort, the needles. She told me about the first, second, third time. How she thought trying might fix her marriage. How she was told Rodrigo's affairs were due to her inability to conceive. How for years, her life became a series of doctor's appointments. How the biggest lesson of being a wife is not learning how to give but learning how to ignore. Ignore you have nothing left to give.

When I'm closing the fence behind her, the girl turns to me, long lashes sweeping her face. With a timid voice she says, "*Mi abuelita.*"

* * *

Aunt Ruth and I look at Sevilla from her rooftop balcony. I see large church crosses, people walking home with their animals, lights flickering around the parish like a silent language. The mountains are enveloped by feather-like stars.

"I want to build a house here," I tell my aunt. She puts her arm around my shoulders. The black threads of her poncho brush against me. She's going to the wake with Rodrigo, to pay their respects to the girl's grandmother. She doesn't invite me, assumes I'm not interested, and I do not ask to go.

I hear chants of *el ave maria* coming from the top of the hill as I sit on the balcony. I can't stop thinking of the little girl's round cheeks, her pain evident from the slump of her shoulders. Her white sneakers running, running away from me after she told me about her grandmother's death. I can't stop thinking of this little girl as a different version of myself if I had grown up in Sevilla de Oro. When my grandmother died, I would be just like her, and I would at least know the rest of the words of the prayer.

* * *

Another myth, this time of a field called Sinchahuasin, near Pujilí. Farmers used to walk past it on their way home after a long day's work. One day, many of them saw a majestic, white-feathered bird with a beak the color of gold. It very nearly blinded them with its beauty and when someone tried to go near it, it disappeared.

A humble farmer who often walked by the field saw the bird, ran after it, and was able to trap it. She went home with the bird and *la guardó* or put it away. The next day, when she went to check on it, she saw it had disappeared. The next week, the woman died.

* * *

Every night when I'm at Aunt Ruth's house, my mother reminds me to lock the bedroom door. Some nights it's a text, other nights a call. "Do *not*," she had emphasized before I left for Ecuador, "under *any* circumstance, be alone with him." Her warnings anger me, make me resentful. There has to be more about Rodrigo that she knows and just won't tell me. Also, I know she remembers that summer night, but she planned my stay with them anyway.

Sometimes, I let the most destructive part of me take over. I want something to happen to me, so I can show it to my mother, like a bruise, a scar, as something I'd be proud of. Almost like, *Look, you could have told me the truth. You could have and you didn't and look at what happened to me because of it.* Another part of me is just curious. I've romanticized Ecuador, and especially Sevilla de Oro, my entire life, but I know it's because I haven't grown up here, and that I would feel differently if I had. I need to know what secrets lie within this small town almost as a way to justify my apprehension. I stare at the unlocked door across from me.

* * *

Aunt Ruth and I attend the military parade in Sevilla de Oro commemorating their independence as well as the decisive Battle of Pichincha that liberated Quito from Spanish control. As the troops march through the center of town, she tells me to stand up straight, that the entire community is involved: the cheerleaders from the local high school perform, young children dance to a *cabalgata* with their toy horses, even taxi drivers honk and roll down their windows and wave as they drive through the crowd. Since I'm a newcomer, it is natural for people to stare, and I do not flinch when they do.

When we're back in Aunt Ruth's home, Rodrigo turns on the television to watch the parade in the Historic Center of Quito, where many Ecuadorian singers perform. I listen to many versions of "*Avecilla*," an Ecuadorian song I've known the lyrics to ever since I can remember: a song about a little bird, captured and forced to be a human's company.

I am anxious for my cousins to arrive for our family reunion with my grandmother's keys so I can finally go inside her house and explore. When they do, they block the streets with their cars. I hug my cousins from Quito, from Cuenca, from el Oriente. Some of them get busy setting up a stereo and we dance on the land and karaoke for the whole town. Aunt Ruth sings "*Avecilla, Amarguras*," another version of the song, except in this one, the human laments the bird's death.

My cousins buy beer from multiple little convenience stores in Sevilla and by midnight, there isn't any beer left in the town, so they start serving hard liquor. We all drink from the same cup. I learn denying a drink is a personal offense and the consequence is to drink double, one on your own and one with whomever you've offended.

When it gets dark, we lead the pig that will feed us tomorrow from the truck to my grandmother's land. I feel its eyes on me. It starts to rain so Aunt Ruth opens the front door of my grandmother's house and my cousins rush in without question. They don't understand my hesitance, that finally, I'll be able to walk into this house.

The house doesn't look abandoned, but rather like someone went away on vacation. There's a bed to my left, next to the entrance, and it's not even made. There are religious figurines of saints on every windowsill, every table, every shelf. The walls are adorned with crosses and prayer plaques. It's just as Catholic as I imagined it would be.

I wonder about the last night my grandmother sat on this bed staring at the night sky with full consciousness. The last night before the memory loss overtook her: what did she do and who did she speak to and what secrets did she think of. I wonder about the nights when the memory loss began, how she must have stared out the window, how she must have paced around the living room thinking of what she had said or what she had done in the hours her mind could no longer hold.

I see the bathroom door slightly ajar. I walk in and put my hands on the light-blue wallpaper. I trace the beautiful outlines of branches and flowers and birds, birds of all species sketched on the wall. Aunt Ruth knocks on the door. When I step out, she places a blanket into my hands, a ball of yarn still attached to a corner. "This is yours," she says. "She didn't get the chance to finish it."

* * *

We dance so much the land sinks. I keep making eye contact with the pig tied to my grandmother's fence. My cousins have decided to kill the pig at dawn. I sit on the edge of the sidewalk by myself, hoping the cold mountain air will sober me. One of my cousins finds me, and in his drunkenness, he props himself next to me. It's quiet for a long moment.

"I heard her die." I let my sentence hang between us. I want to tell him about the sound she made, the birds, the dreams, the old man who grunted at the word *Tía*, the myths I've read about, but I have had too much to drink to form the words and my mouth doesn't move.

"If they don't do anything about it soon, the town is going to take the land away," he whispers. He positions himself so he is now sitting in front of me. He looks conflicted, but he sighs and gets up in a way that makes me dizzy and leaves me confused. After a while, I go back to dancing with the rest of my cousins, but I can't stop thinking about his reaction, how there must be something he wanted to say.

In the morning, I ask my cousin if he'll walk around the town with me. The rest of our family is too tired or too drunk to notice we are gone. I look at him, pointedly.

"What do you know?" I ask. My cousin puts both of his hands on my shoulders and waits until I meet his gaze. He grabs my hand and kisses the back of it like an apology.

"I can't tell you," he says.

"I know more than you think," I am quick to respond.

"What do you know?" he replies, his brows knitting.

"I know that Rodrigo is trying to direct how the inheritance is divided and Ruth isn't even supposed to receive any part of it." I tell him about the sound, the birds, the dreams, the myths. I tell him I know there is something I had to figure out, that there is something inside all of these stories we've heard, something in the past that can change our future, and he gives in.

"When she got sick and everyone started talking about inheritance, my father told me Ruth *no es tía*. Abuelita must have had an affair. He made me swear I'd never tell anyone." He whispers and looks conflicted, like he just tipped the world with his tongue. "But you know Abuelita wouldn't have wanted it that way. Taking everything away from her daughter is not the answer."

And then he adds, concerned, hands still on my shoulders, "If Rodrigo did anything to you...just say the word. Say the word because a lot of people want him dead."

I take a step back and his arms fall to his sides. I do not want to tell him anything about Rodrigo. I had not realized. I guess it didn't quite click until now, that uncovering the past might have disastrous consequences. My cousin makes me swear I won't say anything to anyone.

* * *

After my cousin confirms the truth, I remember the myth about a man who once found a *gagon* and trapped it in a large jar. When he awoke the next day, he saw the gagon was dead and was then informed that his neighbor, a woman who was having a relationship with her brother-in-law, also died. Her body was a deep black.

Los gagones are like newborn puppies, who form when there are improper relations within family or close-knit groups. They first appear an ash color, but over time their fur becomes *negro fino* or a fine black because they represent the souls of those living in sin. If you find a gagon, you are considered pure of heart.

Years later, the man said, "I got to know the daughter of the sinner, she got married but couldn't have children because they say that is the curse."

* * *

When all of my cousins leave Sevilla de Oro, the land looks bare and spent. I spend my days helping Aunt Ruth with her animals. One day, as I try to lure Aunt Ruth's chicken back to her side of the land with pieces of corn I find near her guinea-pig pen, the sun begins to set. The chicken follows, eating the bits I throw as I walk backward. We're almost halfway back when I bump into someone. I turn and it's Rodrigo. His laughter scares the chicken away.

Rodrigo says he still needs to walk up to the fields to feed the cows. He says it would be so much easier to take care of their animals if they were closer to their house, says he hopes they divide the land soon. He wants to put it to good use. When I ask about the bloody rag on his hand, he tells me it's from a machete blade. He was helping a neighbor harvest. Blood drips on the sidewalk between us.

That evening, in the kitchen, as my aunt smiles at us over her shoulder, not really looking, concentrated on the potatoes she's cutting for lunch, I feel Rodrigo's arm wrap around my shoulders. I feel it lower all the way down my back. He grabs me, his head turning for a kiss. I cough loudly in his face.

"Are you okay?" My aunt turns to me, and immediately, Rodrigo's hands leave my body. Aunt Ruth reaches her hand to my forehead, checks if I have a fever. I deny any pain, but she still makes me smell *hierbas* from her garden to prevent any sickness. I call my mother that night and she expresses her disapproval of Rodrigo, but mostly blames me. I go to bed that night in tears, shaken that Rodrigo so boldly touched me while his wife was only a couple feet away from us. Aunt Ruth brings me more blankets, *para que no te agarre el chiflón*, still worried that I am sick. It's rumored that the bird of the Huacay Siqui takes advantage of those who are cold and will play little jokes on the body.

*   *   *

My Aunt Ruth is the most generous person I know. She served me breakfast in bed, hand-washed my clothes, knit for me, waited on me hand and foot. She gives animals and food to the less fortunate in Sevilla de Oro, often invites people to take what they need from her garden. She makes clothes for children with her sewing machine and her crochet. She gives and gives and doesn't complain. She gave me a blanket she confessed she would have given to her daughter if she had had one. I know how much she wants a daughter, and this makes me feel so loved, but also so guilty, because I think of the story of the gagon and I feel like with everything I've learned I've betrayed her. I'm not sure if my Aunt Ruth knows about my grandmother's affair and I couldn't possibly ask her without creating a huge problem for her and the rest of my family. Even if I said something for the purpose of the inheritance, all she would be left with is Rodrigo, a man who she gives and gives to, but who hasn't treated her well.

After our reunion, when it's time for me to leave Sevilla de Oro and head back to New York, I find Rodrigo reading *El Universo*, one of the largest daily newspapers in Ecuador. He tells me about an outraged letter admonishing the Ecuadorian government for tarnishing the military parade. *El Universo* discovered that "Avecilla" was originally written by a Colombian. Rodrigo tells my Aunt Ruth about it as he organizes my suitcases in his truck and they both laugh in shock at a revelation that they weren't searching for, much like me. The song is now ruined for them.

"Thank you for letting me stay here," I tell them both.

"This is your home," Aunt Ruth replies.

It is too silent in the car. I roll down the window just for some noise. I don't want to forget how the cold mountain air feels against my cheeks. I see my reflection in the window and for a moment, I see my grandmother's face and I think of the nights she must have stared at the sky, the starlight, when she realized she was pregnant with another man's child. She must have been so afraid. Every day, she must have suffered with the truth. I don't know what happened, but I do know she must have experienced a lot of silence—that secret, that story, bulging within her. In the wind, I feel echoes of every place, every person, those I've longed to meet and know, those I've loved long before that, of every bird I've seen and read about. I feel a warmth settle within me. We are all made up of stories and that has to be enough.

* * *

Now, when I think of my grandmother, when I think of Aunt Ruth, I think of the myth of Iwia. Iwia was a terrible demon, who would capture the Shuar, put them in his *shigra* or bag, and eat them. This is how he caught Etsa's parents. Iwia believed Etsa was powerful, so he tricked Etsa into thinking he was his son. Every morning, Etsa went into the forest to trap birds for the insatiable Iwia. He would come back with a shigra full of birds of all species, but one day the forest was silent. Yapankam was the only bird left.

"Are you going to kill me, too?" he asked.

"No," Etsa replied. "What would it serve me? I have left the rainforest empty of birds. This silence is terrible."

Etsa sat with Yapankam and as they watched the monkeys and the insects, they became friends. Yapankam told him the truth about his parents and Etsa denied his story, but the more Yapankam spoke, the more Etsa felt the truth settle in his bones. And then, as if a lightning bolt struck him, Etsa *se deshizo en un largo lamento* or fell apart in a long lament.

"Etsa, you can't do anything to bring your parents back to life, but you can bring the birds back to life."

"How?" Etsa replied.

"Put the feathers of all the birds you have killed in your blowgun," Yapankam explained.

The young boy did exactly as he was told and blew into his gun. Immediately, millions of birds took flight. Birds of all colors and species began to fly in the forest and circled around their beloved Etsa.

CHELSY DIAZ AMAYA *is an MFA candidate in Creative Writing and Literature at Stony Brook University. Her work has previously appeared in The Southampton Review.*

On Writing Into What We Don't Know

Robert Glick

The Masters Review Vol. VII, "Questions for Anesthesiologists," selected by Rebecca Makkai

If you worked as an IT Director for anesthesiologists, you might have dressed up in a bunny suit in order to enter the OR. Perhaps it was the seventh hour of a craniotomy; perhaps the anesthesiologist wanted to discuss a revision to a backup schema. In the labs, the researchers might have taught you about Mount Everest or explained caudal blocks while you watched the EKG-wired mice desperately scratching their feet on their clear tubes. If you really paid attention, you'd observe their quest for anesthesiology's Holy Grail: that if we understood how and why anesthetics operated, we'd learn how the brain works.

In the feedback loop of hypothesis, experiment, and result, and through their provisional conversions of magic into science, anesthesiologists propel themselves into what they don't know. There's a marvelous *becoming into understanding* in not knowing a result in advance, in incorporating failure, critique, and rethinking as intrinsic to the project.

The same, I think, is true for writers. We engender the possibility of meaningful becoming. By virtue of our imaginative faculties, stuck in our single consciousness, we *write into what we don't know*. It's not really a choice. And in doing so, we allow readers to marvel in the physical or mental transformation of a character, a landscape, a plot. In these alchemic languages, we can see our imagined selves; we can understand another as another.

> (Yet there are, as with the anesthesiologist, ethical failures built into the process of experiment. Our biases, our assumptions. Ethical problems within our assumptions of knowing what an other is, thinks, or desires. Despite our most well-meaning attempts, words wound. We simplify, we misrepresent, we evoke tropes of identity, we don't give voice at the right time, to the right characters.
>
> How can we write into what we don't know while minimizing the suffering of our readers?
>
> Especially in my subject position, as a straight white cis man who has profited from the writing and publishing worlds, I'm not at all suggesting that writing into what you don't know means that you are free to write whatever you want. Others have written complex, difficult, important works exploring how, when, and why the desire to write/represent/inhabit other personas is complicated by identity; how this writing is always anchored by the limitations of one's own subject position; how one has to consider so delicately whose story to tell and how to tell it.)

I want to suggest that writing into what we don't know isn't simply about content; it must also encompass our treatment of language and structure. For me, the intensity of emotionally powerful *realist* stories is diminished by conventional uses of structure and language, by linear time and straightforward syntax. If, as I believe, every fiction is a gluey accretion of language projecting into possible worlds, and each formal structure maps the shape and contours of each possible world (novel as apartment building

[Georges Perec], story as the chambers of a revolver [Antonya Nelson], language splitting into multiple rows and columns on the page [Toni Morrison and Salvador Plascencia]), then why build a tract home for your beautifully terrifying stories?

I'm not speaking here, as Cathy Park Hong points out, about the avant-garde as an excuse to abnegate responsibility, because one has the privilege of thinking of writing as a space of pure play. I'm thinking more about Dorothy Allison and Bhanu Kapil—a constant distending of language capable of representing the horrors of our daily lives as well as our myriad joys and pleasures, that can deform and reform structures to help understand our individual lives imbricated within conduits and networks and systems.

In "Questions for Anesthesiologists," which was graciously published by *The Masters Review*, there were three ways I hoped to write into what I didn't know. The story is a first-person narration from the perspective of Grace, an anesthesiologist who has just had a miscarriage. Second, on the level of language, I had to locate the incomplete sentences and lyric passages that seemed essential for Grace's character. And lastly, the story is written in semi-linear fashion, using catechism as format. Here, I wanted Grace to be her own interlocutor, so that she can "live outside and inside and outside [her]self, act as one's own ghost and ghostwriter, [her] own language passing through [her] as a hand punches through mist." I'm incredibly grateful for *The Masters Review*, who allowed space for the possibility of this meaningful becoming, despite my failings, the story's failures of empathy and biased projection. May we all write, and have space for these glimmers of lightness of language in relation to trauma. May we all construct startling and uneasy language-buildings: structure as Ferris wheel, minimall, vomitorium.

ROBERT GLICK *is Associate Professor of English at the* Rochester Institute of Technology, *where he teaches creative writing and digital literature. His work has appeared in* The

Normal School, Denver Quarterly, Black Warrior Review, *and* The Gettysburg Review. *His first book,* Two Californias, *was published by* C&R Press *in 2019.*

Atlas, Bayonet, (War) Correspondence: An Abecedarian

Tanya Bellehumeur-Allatt

Atlas (*noun*)

1 : a Titan of Greek mythology often represented as bearing the heavens on his shoulder; one who bears a heavy burden
2 : a bound collection of maps

I curl the ends of my braids around my fingers. "How far away is it?"

"I'll show you." Maman leaves the room and comes back with the enormous family atlas.

"We're here." She puts her finger on Great Slave Lake, an easy find at the top of North America. From there, she slides her finger to the right, over the Atlantic Ocean and Europe until it stops on a country the size of a slivered almond.

Israel.

> **Bayonet** (*noun*)
>
> **1** : a steel blade made to be attached to the muzzle end of a shoulder arm; used especially for slashing and stabbing in hand-to-hand combat

My father stops the car at a checkpoint. A guard in combat fatigues points his machine gun at the sandbags and pylons blocking the road. The spike-shaped bayonet fastened to the gun's muzzle catches the light of the setting sun and gleams.

My father rolls down his window and flashes his ID card, then gestures toward us. "I'm travelling with my wife, my fourteen-year-old son, and my twelve-year-old daughter. We're with the UN."

There is no Canadian equivalent for this—no neat conversion, like shekels to dollars. I can't take my eyes off the bayonet's metal point.

> **Correspondence** (*noun*)
>
> **1** : the state or condition of agreement of one thing with another
> **2** : communication between persons by an exchange of letters

Tiberias, Israel
September 1982

Dear Mrs. Blackwood,

Atmospheric conditions here make it impossible for me to conduct the bean growth experiment as outlined in the science manual for this month.

Sincerely,

I sign my name in a curly, fancy way and stuff the letter into the bulging envelope full of this week's school papers. Then I cradle the hard beans in my hand and shoot them, one by one, like smooth tiddlywinks, out the center of the screenless porch-door window, through the narrow balcony, into the air beyond. On the wall of my room, two transparent lizards blink at me: a gesture of solidarity from the natural world.

> **Dependent** (*noun*)
>
> **1** : one that depends; person unable to care for herself
>
> **Note:** Military dependents are the spouse, children, and possibly other relationship categories of a sponsoring military member for purposes of pay as well as special benefits, privileges, and rights
>
> **Dependapotamus** (*noun*) [*Urban Dictionary*]
> **Dependapotami** (*plural noun*)
>
> **1** : the spouse or child of a military service member whose symbiotic relationship is parasitic

It's the middle of the afternoon. My father is away, but my mother is pouring tea for a United Nations officer in our living room.

"As you are well aware," the officer says, "four peacekeepers were killed by a land mine earlier this month when they pulled their jeep over to the side of the road." He breaks a digestive cookie in two and stuffs it into his mouth. "Outside Beirut."

"Molly O'Shaunessey is a friend of mine. I was with her when she heard the news." My mother balances her teacup on her lap.

"We asked for volunteers to take their place in Beirut and your husband came forward. He'll be the operations officer."

Maman sets her cup on the glass coffee table. She stares at the uneaten cookie on the saucer. "When will he begin?"

"As soon as possible." The man fills the silence by eating another cookie.

"*Et nous?*" It is as though, for a moment, my mother has forgotten the man is sitting there. "*La guerre civile... les bombardements... Impossible de se trouver un appartement.*" She looks up from her cup. "Where will we live?"

"You cannot follow him there. Think of the danger." The man stands. "I must be on my way... Thank you for the lovely tea." He fiddles with the Velcro band of his wristwatch while my mother stares at her palms as if trying to decipher her future. "I'll see myself out."

> **Efrat** (*noun*)
>
> **1** : an Israeli settlement established in 1983 in the Judean mountains of the West Bank. Efrat is located 12 km south of Jerusalem, between Bethlehem and Hebron, inside the Security Barrier
> **2** : a Hebrew girl's name, meaning 'fruitful'

Efrat is fourteen and has lived in Israel all her life. "Born here," she says, as if that gives her special importance. Unlike the other girls in our apartment building, her hair is short—parted on the side and pushed back behind the ears, where it curls around her face. She wears pants instead of the traditional long skirts of the Orthodox community.

"Who are you?" she asks me with a throaty Hebrew accent. "Where do you come from?"

"Canada." My brother, Etienne, points at the maple leaf on the front of his shirt. My father told us to sew Canadian badges on our backpacks. He gave us stickers for our suitcases and pins for our hats and coats. Our country, he says, is a friend to all the nations—not like the US, France, or Russia, who take sides when there's a fight.

Efrat takes in our jeans and T-shirts, my Mickey Mouse watch and braids. She points to my father's blue beret on a hook near the door. "United Nations?" She makes a hippie peace sign with her fingers.

When I tell her we're moving to Beirut, her eyes grow round. Her brother is serving there, with the Israeli Defense Forces.

"I'll write to you." It's what I always say when it's time to say goodbye to my friends.

"No." Efrat shakes her head. "Don't write to me. It's not allowed."

> **Flyway** (*noun*)
>
> : The Rift Valley/Red Sea Flyway includes the Jordan Valley down through Syria, Lebanon, Jordan, and Israel. It is one of the biggest in the world, with over one and a half million soaring birds flying through it every year. The flyway links the European breeding grounds with the African wintering areas of migrating birds.
>
> — United Nations Development Program/ Migratory Soaring Birds Project

In my sixth-grade science class in Yellowknife, we'd studied birds. At the end of the unit, each student had to build a nest. Our teacher, Mrs. Nouger, had said a nest should offer reprieve, refuge, and rejuvenation. She'd encouraged us to use any kind of material we wanted, and to have it express our deepest notion of home.

For my project, I'd lined my nest with a drawing of our pink house on Gitzel Street with our forested backyard that led all the way to the lake. I'd cut up the sheet music I'd memorized for our recorder-ensemble recital at the sixth-grade graduation and added photographs of me with my best friend, Catherine.

My family is like the geese and cranes Mrs. Nouger taught us about, that fly away at the change of every season, constantly on their way to someplace else, never stopping for long, always looking for a better place to land.

> **Green Line** (*noun*)
>
> **1** : demarcation line between Muslim west Beirut and Christian east Beirut

Apartments and storefronts stare back at me through empty, black eye sockets. The abandoned buildings are held up with sandbags and surrounded by barbed wire.

My parents stand beside a sapling tree that pushes its way between broken slabs of pavement on either side of the demarcation line. Maman points at a vine growing up the façade of a dilapidated, bombed-out building. "Morning glory. It must be drinking the acid in the rust."

The street makes me think of the scene in *Sleeping Beauty*, when Aurora is woken from her hundred-year sleep and her ruined castle has been transformed into a lush, green garden.

On either side is destruction. But all along the line separating the city into Muslim west and Christian east: trees, shrubs, and wildflowers grow—an astonishing sight amidst all the ruin.

> **Holiday** (*noun*)
>
> **1** : a good time; a festive occasion

Beirut, under siege since June, is now in a state of emergency: a hotbed of revolt, dissension, murders, and kidnappings so dangerous that our parents decide to take us away for a week, maybe more.

"We're fleeing to Egypt, like the Holy Family," Maman says while we pack our bags in the night. We take the first flight out of Beirut.

I've grown up with stories about my father's UN tours in Cairo. He's talked about Egypt as if it were a mythical place where you can fry an egg on the sidewalk and have a mushroom grow out of your forehead.

Now we're here, with him, and I want to be impressed. But I can't make myself care about mummified cats and pharaohs. All I want to do is watch HBO movies on the hotel TV. Rest my head on the clean, white pillowcase. Order room service. Eat strawberries. I can't handle any more pain, misery, or tragedy.

But my parents want to explore.

I (*pronoun*)

1 : the first person singular; the one who is speaking or writing

*"Farewell to you and the youth I have spent with you.
It was but yesterday we met in a dream."*
—KHALIL GIBRAN, *The Prophet*

When we leave Canada, I am a child.
One year later, when we return, I am an adult.

Jeep (*noun*)

1 : multipurpose motor vehicle

My father takes us to Sabra and Shatila—Palestinian camps in southern Beirut—one evening after supper.

He switches the radio to a French news channel and turns up the volume as we drive away from the coast.

We pass a UN checkpoint and enter through a gate. Cement walls topped with embedded glass shards and razor wire surround the enclosure.

My father slows the jeep to a crawl. The wind that whipped the UN flag a few minutes earlier has died. The flag hangs limply. My father flicks on the jeep's high beams, showing two massive piles of dirt on either side of the entrance. Farther on, I can make out cinderblock houses with red graffiti spray-painted across them in undecipherable Arabic.

"What's with the huge piles of dirt?" Etienne asks.

Maman keeps her head down. She fiddles with her hair.

"Those are mass graves," my father says.

The radio announcer drones on about soccer championships in clipped European French.

"Turn that off," my mother snaps. She presses buttons on the jeep's console, but the radio keeps playing. Finally, she finds the volume button.

"Thirty-five hundred people were killed here in September," my father says. "Mostly women and children and the elderly." He drives the jeep forward. I try not to imagine the bodies piled up under the layers of sand and mud.

The narrow street—barely wide enough for our jeep—is littered with garbage. The houses are dark. On the side of one I make out the English words: *Sabra and Shatila Massacre. September 1982.*

"It took place over three days," my father says. "The fighters used military flares at night to help them see."

"Who did it?" Etienne asks.

"No one has claimed responsibility," my father says. "But we suspect Lebanese Phalangists. With help from the IDF."

"That's enough," Maman says. "Take us back."

But the road is too narrow. There is no place for the jeep to turn around.

Knife (*noun*)

1 : a simple instrument used for cutting

In Yellowknife, my father equipped us each with a Swiss Army knife. Maman's was small, with only a few appendages—a pair of scissors, a couple of blades, a file. She kept it in her purse until it was confiscated by an El Al attendant in plastic gloves before we boarded our flight for Tel Aviv.

My brother's knife is the fat one—fully loaded—with every sort of blade and gadget, including the can opener and the white toothpick.

My knife is the version in between Maman's and Etienne's. I carry it with me every day in a special zipper pouch in my schoolbag. Some day one of the Lebanese guards stationed outside the American Embassy gates, next to the tank, will find it. He'll feel it against the polyester fabric, undo the zipper with curious fingers, and lift it from its special place. But most mornings, it's the same two guards. They recognize us. We show them our ID cards, they unzip our bags and give them a cursory pat, flip through a schoolbook or two, and wave us on.

Until recently, I've used my knife to cut loose threads on my jeans or make paper snowflakes. On a camping trip on Great Slave Lake, I used my knife to whittle a branch for a marshmallow stick. But Friday afternoon, while the other girls are doing basketball drills in the gym, I lock myself in a bathroom stall and take my knife out of my bag.

I choose the largest, sharpest blade. I roll my sleeve to my elbow, turn my left wrist and open my palm, run my thumb over the thin flesh.

Bring the blade down hard. I need to feel the sharp pain, need to see the bright drops of blood fall on the toilet seat.

It's harder than I imagined. The skin resists. Human flesh is harder to whittle than wood.

I press the blade. Hold my breath. Listen to the pounding of the basketball against the gym floor, the whistle—two short blows and a longer one—followed by the angry buzzer. They must be playing a game now. How long before the coach notices I'm missing? I want him to leave the game and come looking for me, but I know he won't.

I mop up the blood with toilet paper. It sticks to the fresh wound. Unroll my sleeve, pull my hoodie over top. It's too hot for muggy April in Beirut. Too hot for the gym.

I leave the stall, look out the bathroom window at the four American warships in the bay with their cannons pointed at the city. Pointed at the school. Pointed at me.

At least I feel something now rather than just the numbness. If I stop feeling, if I catch myself slipping back, all I have to do is press hard on the inside of my wrist.

Next time, I'll cut deeper. It'll be easier, now that I know what to do.

Library (*noun*)

1 : building given over to books

I'm sitting alone in the library at Beirut's American Community School, reading. I enjoy spending my free period in the stacks, an oasis of quiet in the middle of my day.

Suddenly there's a deafening boom, a sound louder than I've ever heard before. Everything shakes. The room goes black. Books fall off the shelves. The chairs next to me roll over. A window cracks and splits, sending shards flying.

My breath comes loud and ragged. Voices shout in Arabic. I don't know what they are saying, or what to do, so I stay in my seat and wait for my eyes to adjust to the cavernous dark.

Sirens blare. Panic simmers in my chest, threatens to choke me.

I sit for a long time, listening to the chaos, until my French teacher finds me and leads me to his classroom with a flashlight. We conjugate French verbs by candlelight until we learn the news. A bomb has exploded at the American Embassy next door.

At 3:30, when the bell rings and it's time to go home, red DANGER tape encircles the school.

> **Missing** (*adjective*)
>
> **1** : not able to be found; not present; absent without explanation from one's home or usual or expected place

My mother answers the door on my father's birthday, heaving its thick, bullet-proof bulk open to find a grim messenger. Daddy is lost—caught in the cross fire—missing in action.

Daddy is dead. Dead. He won't be coming home again. Ever.

A few hours later, we hear the lock turn. The front door opens. "A hot bath and bed," my father says, as if speaking to himself.

We stare at him. My mouth fills with hot, dry air and makes my body light.

"*T'étais où?*" Anger tinges Maman's voice.

Daddy takes off his glasses and wipes his face with his hands. He shuts the door behind him. "I got caught behind enemy lines. My partner wanted to go farther, to see what was behind the barricade. I never should have agreed…"

> **Neutral** (*adjective*)
>
> **1** : not engaged on either side; not siding with or assisting either of two or more contending parties; not involved in hostilities

"What kind of weapons do you have out there?" Etienne asks. "Pistols? Revolvers?"

"It's against the rules," Daddy says. "Blue Berets don't carry arms."

> **Orient** (*verb*)
>
> **1** : to ascertain the bearings of; to set right by adjusting to facts or principles; put into correct position or relation

In geography class, we memorize all the main American rivers, their sources and tributaries. We recite the Preamble to the Constitution. "*We the People of the United States, in Order to form a more perfect Union, establish Justice, ensure domestic Tranquility, provide for the common defense. . .*"

We also learn the points of the compass, how to read a map and orient ourselves. None of this is new to me; orienteering is one of my father's passions. On camping trips in Yellowknife, he taught us to tell time by making a sundial in the sand. We took turns finding our way back to our campground, through the forest, by using a compass and a topographical map.

In Beirut, every day, we walk to school along the route my father drew for us when we arrived. It's a circuitous, hour-long path, since there are areas of the city we have to avoid. Etienne and I are to remain together at all times. Never deviate from the path. Come directly home.

> **Passport** (*noun*)
>
> **1** : enables the bearer to exit and reenter their country freely. If necessary, requests protection for the bearer while abroad
>
> **Note:** Since 11 December 2001, Canadian children have not been included in parents' passports, and passports have been issued for one person only.

On a weekend trip to Damascus, Maman and Etienne each have their passports on strings around their necks, tucked under their shirts. If I disappear, I don't have any official documents except my name printed on a card inside my backpack.

I receive a marriage proposal while walking through the souk—camels and gold in exchange for me. I'd be the third wife of a man in a creased black-and-white photo pulled from beneath the burqa of a woman who stands in a narrow doorway. At twelve, I'm old enough to marry her son.

> **Quest** (*noun*)
>
> **1** : expedition; pursuit; venture, usually involving an adventurous journey
>
> **Quest(ion)** (*noun*)
>
> **1** : an inquiry; a subject or aspect that is in dispute; something the correctness or existence of which is open to doubt
>
> **Risk** (*noun*)
>
> **1** : the possibility of loss, injury, disadvantage, or destruction; contingency, danger, peril, threat

Johan spreads his hand-drawn Risk game on the table. The countries are labeled in large block letters, next to their respective flags. Inside the countries, in blue ink, he's drawn caricatures of all the United Nations kids.

My caricature features long braids, glasses, shaggy bangs, and large teeth. Hardly flattering, but not bad for a freestyle drawing with a ballpoint pen. If it had been drawn a year earlier, my teeth would have been crooked, leaning awkwardly against one another like slats of a broken fence.

Next to me, my brother grins and flexes huge biceps under his Mr. Universe T-shirt, a maple leaf tattooed on his forearm.

Disembodied arms reach out to grab us from the edges of the continents.

> **Soldier's Heart** (*noun*)
>
> **1** : term coined during the American Civil War to denote a psychological response to the experience of intense traumatic events, particularly those that threaten life. Also known as 'shell shock' in WWI, 'war neurosis' in WWII, 'combat stress reaction' during the Vietnam War, and Post-Traumatic Stress Disorder, beginning in 1980
>
> **Note:** Despite the prevalence of 'soldier's heart,' no psychological support was given to Canadian peacekeepers in combat zones, or to their families, until 1987, following Canada's peacekeeping endeavors in Sarajevo and the former Yugoslavia.

Once this year is over, we'll be expected to settle into our new lives as if we've just come from a regular military posting at some other army base in Canada, like Valcartier or Petawawa. No matter that we've come from a theater of war.

> **Twilight Status** (*noun*)
>
> **1** : a legally recognized temporary status; an in-between state

When well-meaning people ask, "Where are you from?" I don't know what to say.
"Where did you live before?"
"In Yellowknife, in the Northwest Territories."
"Cool. You're from the Arctic."
"Well, no. I just lived there for three years."
"Where were you born?"
"Germany."
"Oh. You're German."
"No. I'm Canadian."

To French Canadians, I am English. To the English, I am French.

I study and read in English. My French is domestic, rarely spoken outside our home. It's my cradle language, but it's patchy and quirky, with lots of awkward pauses while I translate in my head.

All I want is a geography to call my own.

> **USD** (*noun*)
>
> **1** : American currency, often accepted in other countries as well as in the United States

"At the back of the fridge," my father says, "in a cookie tin, are ten thousand US dollars. If ever the fighting gets so bad that we need to leave in a hurry, and the airport is closed, we'll use the money to hire a rowboat to take us across the Mediterranean." He looks me full in the face. "I want you to know that. Just in case."

> **Vacate** (*verb*)
>
> **1** : to make useless, ineffectual, or without significance
> **2** : to go away, to leave
> **3** : to take a vacation

"We need to exit through the airport kitchen," my father says in a voice that is too loud and cheerful. We walk in single file between the shiny stainless-steel counters stacked high with prepackaged airplane food on plastic trays. First my father, then my mother, my brother, and finally, me.

I walk quickly, often stepping on my brother's heels as we pass through a corridor of refrigerators, massive, industrial-sized sinks with pyramids of pots waiting to be washed, and cardboard boxes heaped with citrus fruit that give off a rancid smell.

"Quit it," my brother snarls.

"I can't help it," I say softly, not wanting to draw attention to myself. I would hook my fingers through the belt loop of his jeans if he'd let me.

We round a corner and I catch sight of my father, ever the soldier, walking straight and tall: shoulders back, chin forward, as if it is his typical morning routine to march his wife and children through a foreign airport's kitchen.

We push through the last door and step out into the searing heat of the morning sun. It presses down on my head and radiates up from the black tarmac. My eyes sting at the brightness of the light. But there is the small Cessna, with its side door open, ready to fly us over enemy airspace, into Israel. Our suitcases are waiting for us at the bottom of the metal steps.

> **Witness** (*verb*)
>
> **1** : give testimony; provide oral or written evidence of; attest; to see or know by reason of personal presence

Thirty years into the future, when I'm middle aged, the images will still haunt me. I'll feel a responsibility to write it all down. Make it known. Bear witness.

But for now, I stuff it inside. Try my best to forget.

> **X** (*noun*)
>
> **1** : something that is wrong; mistake; error
>
> **YUL** (*noun*)
>
> **1** : Montréal-Trudeau International Airport code

When we land in Montréal, there is no one to meet us. We wouldn't all fit in my grandparents' car, so they've opted to wait for us at home. We pile into a taxi. I press my face to the window, intoxicated with all the green. We're home. Sort of. Back in Canada, at last, but no one seems to take any notice. We have no friends in this city. We're posted to Sherbrooke, an hour and a half away. No friends there, either. But never mind. My parents will buy a house—their first. Etienne and I will go to school. We'll start again. We'll try. Hello, Canada. Hello.

Zero (*adjective*)
1 : relating to, or being a zero
2 : forming a fixed point of departure in reckoning; absent; lacking; belonging to or being a group or class arbitrarily or conveniently designated zero; null; empty

I hang out in the school library, garrisoned by books. I surround myself with words as if they might save me, or at least help me trace a few boundaries. Bring definition.

TANYA BELLEHUMEUR-ALLATT's fiction, essays and poems have appeared in Best Canadian Essays 2019 *and* Best Canadian Essays 2015, The New Quarterly, Grain, EVENT, Prairie Fire, Malahat Review, subTerrain, carte blanche, Antigonish Review, Room, Queens Quarterly *(forthcoming) and* The Toronto Star, *among other publications. She holds an MA from McGill University and an MFA in Creative Writing from UBC. Tanya is the author of the poetry collection* Chaos Theories of Goodness *and* Peacekeeper's Daughter: A Middle East Memoir.

Read more about Tanya and her writing at https://tanyaallatt bellehumeur.com

Sugar

Francis Walsh

I lived alone on the hem of a bell-shaped lake in the Maine woods. Pine shrub and birch surrounded the land, and it was quite nice, although it had taken me some time to clear the area of debris left over from the wood-bound parties that the locals had thrown over the years. Water-warped cardboard and swollen cigarette butts littered the ground, and I swept it all away into black trash bags that filled and sprouted like moles along the side of my house. I built the house myself, first burrowing beneath a rocky outcropping and then reenforcing the dirt walls with wood salvaged from the nearby municipal waste station. Down at the station, the stenciling on the waste trucks featured the town seal and the town motto, INDUSTRIA, and if I am being honest—and I am often, but not exclusively, sincere and candid—I entered the dump after hours, clambering over the chain-link fence and skulking around the dumpsters in the dark. One might wonder what compelled me to raid the dump at night, but the answer would be obvious if one caught sight of me. Though my parents named me Sugar, the outside world had bestowed me with many other appellations—Sasquatch, Bigfoot, or, as I now preferred, the North American Wood Ape.

*   *   *

Beyond relating the story of my home, I mentioned the municipal waste station with certain intentions.

Like most criminals and interlopers, I had cased the joint, hiding in the brush with a pair of binoculars some yards away. It was autumn, and my coloration—amber and tobacco—provided natural camouflage as I huddled among the papery leaves, watching trucks trundle into the facility and deposit refuse into the hopper that compressed everything with a satisfying crunch. Men and women in orange safety vests loitered and sipped coffee from paper cups, and ribbons of steam drifted upward in the cold. Once, everyone cheered when a young man named Ronnie—I was close enough to hear someone call his name—arrived with a bag of donuts that filled the group of workers with exclamations of delight. And though it shames me to say, after I watched Ronnie crumple the bag and lob it into a trash bin—there were more cheers, for Ronnie moved with the lithe grace of a former high school basketball player—I waited until nightfall, snuck into the dump, and removed the donut bag from the trash can. First, I inhaled, and the bag shrank up against my face, and then I licked a finger and dabbed the plastic for crumbs. I closed my eyes as a sugary morsel of chocolate bloomed on my tongue, and I experienced a revelation of sorts—if I could be anything at all, I would be a sanitation worker if only so I could work alongside Ronnie and receive his gifts.

*   *   *

But who would hire a North American Wood Ape? I was aware of the curiosity people expressed about me. I was a hermit in the woods, except during winter when the cold afforded me a pretense for wearing a ski mask and gloves and snowsuit to obscure my hair and broad forehead. The fabric of the snowsuit swished between my thighs whenever I walked into town. It's difficult being alone all the time. I had relatives scattered across the country, but reunions were difficult. Certainly, the disguise did nothing for my height, but often people disregarded a singular incongruity—an exceptionally tall person at a café might go unnoticed, but an exceptionally tall person who refused to remove their ski mask indoors might turn heads and force whispers of concern. For this reason, I tended to gulp my coffee.

But I relished the brief interactions I had with people, sometimes to my detriment: the long walk into town provided me with ample opportunity to imagine different possible exchanges with Francine, the barista at the café, from the traditional "How are you today?" to something more colloquial like "It's colder than a witch's tit out there." (I preferred to imagine the colloquial because I always hoped for a belly laugh from crooked-toothed Francine.) But often when I stepped through the café door—the bell chiming above my head as I ducked—my tongue tied itself into knots and I mumbled my order. In many ways I envied Francine. She was free from the unwieldy appurtenances of my own disguise and wore many different outfits—overalls and turtleneck sweaters, leggings and dresses—but never a ski mask, and she was bright and pleasant with a round face and round eyes and a round bob of hair that she brushed behind her ears.

On rare occasions when I lingered and drank my coffee in the café, leaning against the counter, nodding to any other nearby customers, I often caught glimpses of Francine reading. Once, she had her face buried in the gutter of a textbook, and I managed to croak: "Studying?" To which she flashed her crooked smile and held up the text: nursing. And my heart swelled to imagine this young woman planning her future because I too dreamed of my future.

Sometimes my exchanges with the café clerk went nowhere, or—and I never blamed her—she would be in a sullen mood and unresponsive. Everyone had a life, but on those days, I would spend the entire walk home cursing my ski mask and my thick tongue and my inability to untangle the misery of a stranger, even as I knew it was not my responsibility. But the need for affection and companionship drives many people into irresponsibility, and I often found myself living on the outside while dreaming of the lush interiors of other people's lives.

* * *

A few words on my appearance: I both fulfilled and ignored the historical representations of the North American Wood Ape. You would recognize yourself in the mythic contours of my face. I had a mother and father, but then, many children have lived long enough to leave behind a cairn of stones and a burial plot, and in this I was not unique, although my mother had often told me I took after my father, which made me feel like an individual, given the circumstances. I took pride in my hair and groomed myself every evening with a comb carved from the antler of a buck that had died long ago. The comb was a gift from my mother.

* * *

After tasting the donut, which I considered a perk of the sanitation worker, I began to spend more time observing the waste depot.

Despite the slow speed with which it moved, the local government occasionally invested in municipal improvements. Such was the case that autumn of my vigilance when the town council introduced new waste receptacles and implemented new protocols for recycling and trash collection. Living in the woods, and quite a way from the main roads, I was outside of the collection routes—but one day while I watched from my blind in the woods, a delivery truck arrived and unloaded countless wheeled recycling bins, all blue. As well, the sanitation workers crowded together to admire a new truck, one specifically designed with a pneumatic arm that raised and lowered the recycling bins, upending the contents into the open-box bed. The workers inspected the bins, lifting the lids and ducking their heads inside, and Ronnie tested the mechanics of the arm, nodding in approval—the new arm eliminated the burden of lifting and dumping the recycling bins, but still required a human hand to affix the bins to the arms, and so Ronnie, I assumed, approved that he and his coworkers had escaped redundancy and extinction, although this may have been a romantic invention of mine—it was impossible for me to be sure of what Ronnie was thinking.

But all afternoon, I considered what Ronnie might be thinking, and I imagined countless scenarios while I nestled among the leaves—I pictured his expression if we ran into each other in the woods and the way his face might retreat, scrunching his chin to his neck—and as I climbed over the waste-station fence that later evening, I considered other woodland tableaus—perhaps we could share a beer around the flickering shadows of a campfire—and as I tossed the new recycling bin over the fence, where it landed with a thud, I thought, well, perhaps Ronnie will run into me one morning while he collects my well-sorted plastics and aluminums.

* * *

On the first morning that I wheeled my recycling bin to the road, I considered the ethics of loneliness. I tried to think in terms of obligations and duties. What was my obligation to my own happiness? Did the deceit and theft of my recycling bin muddy my pursuit? If I were to fill out a dating profile, could I honestly call myself a recycler?

But aside from abstract considerations, I had concrete concerns—I produced little recycling of my own and had spent the preceding week tramping through the woods collecting discarded beer cans that had gone yellow in the sun. Still, on the morning of collection, I marched forward. Dawn light peeked above the horizon as banners of fog unfurled between the trunks of pine trees while I wheeled my recycling bin over the uneven, needle-laden ground toward a road some distance from my home. When I arrived, a row of bins stood ready for collection, and I wheeled my own into position, then scampered into the woods to view from afar. The sun bloomed, warming, and soon the rumble of the truck filled the air, hissing to a stop near my recycling bin, and Ronnie hopped from the back of the truck and began affixing the pneumatic arm to a bin. A clatter of plastic and aluminum drifted to my ears, and finally, Ronnie's voice bounded and echoed up into the trees: "All set!"

The truck drove away, but the full roundness and euphony of Ronnie's words lingered in my head all week. I found myself repeating them aloud in different tones and arrangements—elongated, breathless, staccato, or even as a single word, eliding the gap, and I found myself growing closer to Ronnie, even from so far away.

* * *

Later, I grew more daring, and waited at the end of the road until I heard the truck in the distance, at which point I would slowly trudge toward the other bins, arriving in time to hand Ronnie my recycling.

I was sweating beneath my ski mask, but Ronnie smiled, winked, and said, "Just in time." His gloved hand touched my gloved hand during the exchange.

Up close, Ronnie was taller than I had realized. Nearly as tall as me. And his movements were even more graceful, like the pulse of a breeze, rushing in, subsiding, and rushing in again. When Ronnie wheeled the bin back to me, I had enough time to work the mouth hole of my ski mask into a smile and say, "Thank you."

His eyes rolled over my body, then one of them winked, and he turned and hopped onto the back of the truck as it pulled away. He waved and said, "See you next week."

And I did. And for weeks after that, even when autumn descended into winter and snow and wind pelted the state and the light of dawn never seemed to break. Soon the municipal workers adorned their truck with blinking Christmas lights. They affixed a plastic Santa Claus to the grill, and it was in the darkness of the early morning, as red and green flashes of light colored the snow, that Ronnie asked me why he never saw me in town, a question that he quickly turned into an invitation: "I always hang out at Post 142. I want to see you in town. Stop by sometime."

He was hanging off the back of the truck as he spoke, and he had to yell above the moaning engine, ending his invitation with a promise: "I'll buy you a beer."

* * *

Ronnie and I sat in his truck one night when I caught his eyes glancing into the rearview mirror. The engine idled. We sat at a turnoff on an access road, and the heaters blasted warm air while the windows gathered snowflakes. Of course, I had met him for that beer. And then another. When he asked me my name, and I told him, he responded as many people had before: "Sugar, that's sweet." And though the joke was stale, he brought freshness to the statement with the way the skin around his eyes crinkled with warmth when he smiled.

I never took my mask off, and when he inquired why, I said, "Poor circulation." He seemed to accept my explanation.

At the time I made the explanation, I had picked at the label on my beer until a pile of paper shreds lay atop the bar; I had never thought of myself as a liar before, but now I had told multiple lies—but I also wondered whether desire might trump a lie. I did not mean my desire for Ronnie, who turned out to be a pleasant enough man in his midthirties with an ex-girlfriend and a tow-headed daughter; he had flipped his wallet open on the bar, and there was a photo of all three of them enshrined in the little plastic window: the ex-girlfriend, firm and youthful, and the child, soft and moony, all smiling. He apologized for showing me his ex-girlfriend, and the conversation pivoted to his side-business as a mechanic. But when I said desire, what I meant was, if I desired to be with another person, was it okay to lie, especially if the lies seemed superficial? Of course, I knew I lied because I had accepted a truth: I saw no other avenue into his affection other than through the ruse of recycling and the shield of my mask.

*   *   *

So far, I had refused Ronnie's overtures to accompany him home at the end of the night, which he seemed to find demure.

"Old fashioned. I get it. 'Course I never went that way, but then I have a kid."

He was polite and would drive me to the end of my road. Occasionally, we kissed. His attraction to me was a surprise, but perhaps not how you think. I had never considered myself unattractive. The biggest myth of all myths centered on the outsider's belief is that the monster somehow considers itself monstrous. But really, that seems sapienscentric. Humans invented mirrors and what is a mirror for but inspecting flaws and for the reassurance that the kale is no longer in your teeth?

In the truck, I watched Ronnie watch me in the mirror, and I shivered when he placed a hand on my thigh.

"You know," he said, "Your muscles really turn me on. Your size. That's what I like best about you."

When I walked home after exiting the truck later that evening, I felt the heat of my body boil the air into steam. Alas, entropy—Ronnie had never seen me, not exactly, and so I was surprised at his attraction. Still, the air around my body cooled on the long walk home.

* * *

The next day, I strolled into town. The sun was out, and my thoughts were stuck on Ronnie —along with becoming a liar, I considered the possibility that I had transformed Ronnie. I was not one to rush into romance. While I enjoyed his company, I also had to admit he had his share of shortcomings—he was older than I thought, with a child and a job that, even if it had benefits and decent pay—was entry level. He talked of building his business, but people tend to make boastful conjectures in courtship. In the same way, did my desire for company create a Ronnie that did not exist? Much like how I lied about myself, was Ronnie a mechanic and loving father, or a dreamer with a wallet-sized photo?

And I must have looked pensive, because while I leaned against the counter sipping coffee, I didn't notice Francine sidle up until she said, "Rough day?"

Surprised, I nodded. "How's studying going?"

"I love it. The commute is a chore, and the classes are long, but it's what I want to be doing. I'm going into nursing."

I wiped my mouth with the back of my hand. Coffee wetted my mask.

"Didn't want to take the plunge and be a doctor?"

She wrinkled her nose.

"Doctors don't do shit. Refill?"

I slid my cup toward her, and she continued to talk while she pumped the lever on the carafe.

"My aunt was a nurse. Don't worry, she's not dead. Retired. She always told me people never appreciate their legs until they're broken, and she got to be the person to guide patients out of that moment. Doctors swoop in and diagnose, but day-to-day care—that's the nurse. So, it's been my dream job, I guess. To be helpful. Plus, the bodies are pretty wonderful. So diverse and weird. What about you?"

She placed the coffee in my hands.

"You know," and I found myself stretching the truth, "when I was younger, I wanted to work in sanitation."

"You mean garbage?"

"Yeah, driving the truck, or hanging off the back, tossing bins, that kind of thing. Keeping the area clean."

Francine crossed her arms over her chest and nodded.

"I can see the appeal. Government jobs are pretty stable. They might be hiring, you know. You could always apply. What are you doing for work now?"

Thankfully, the bell above the door rang before I was forced to answer with another lie, so I gulped my coffee, thanked Francine, and hustled out the door, heading toward my home by the lake where the wind-whipped water never forced me into the pose of an applicant interviewing for friendship.

* * *

Eventually it happened with Ronnie. We slept together.

In my experience—I have lived in many areas across the Northeast—people tend to discount the sexual lives of individuals who appear different from themselves, especially if they are outside their area of attraction. I say this because I wish to convey that, limited as my experiences were, they were not nonexistent.

It's easy in the dark, so to speak. And so, when Ronnie and I stumbled into his house—one story, the living room littered with empty beer cans and oily car parts in different stages of disassembly—we made our way to his bedroom, disassembling ourselves along the way. I requested we leave the lights off, and when it was over, he fell asleep. The whisper of his breath filled the room, and I slinked away, gathering my clothes on the way to the door so he would not catch me in the early morning light.

The sex with Ronnie was not unsatisfying, but as I padded through the woods toward my home—still a bit loopy from all the alcohol—I recalled that when I asked Ronnie to leave the lights off, he had mumbled, hoarse and breathless, "That's fine. I don't need to see you. I only need to feel the size of your body. That's what I care about. That's what turns me on."

And I wondered about that.

* * *

I met Ronnie again soon after we had sex. In fact, we had sex a few more times, and though he was drunk when we entangled ourselves, his breath sour in my mouth, I remained sober. In many ways, the encounters were fun and satisfying. He would whisper in my ear, and he would ask me to be on top, and he would talk about my height and the circumference of my thighs—twenty-eight inches, discovered once when we had parked in his driveway and he had popped the glove box and removed a tape measure—and while part of me felt desired, the more he spoke the more the experience seemed mechanical and the more I felt outside of myself and drifted away from the experience.

The last time I met Ronnie, I let him down gently. Perhaps his winsome interactions with his coworkers had befuddled my better judgment, or perhaps I preferred the chase to the goal. Either way, I felt I made the correct decision. Before he said anything, he scrunched his face into a shape I had never seen before and then pounded his fists against the steering wheel of his truck, but in the end, after he had calmed down and allowed his breath to rise and fall in an easy, steady rhythm, he said, "Okay, okay. I understand. Sometimes things don't work out."

I thanked Ronnie for understanding, and, in fact, was quite proud of him for his response. But a week later, and for weeks after that, I would awake to find garbage strewn across my lawn—plastic water bottles, little knotted bundles of dog feces, torn garbage bags that fluttered in the bony fingers of shrubs, and scraps of food that attracted raccoons. Over and over, I cleaned, and at night I walked to the waste depot, the garbage bags slung over my shoulder. I had misjudged Ronnie, or perhaps misread him, but I knew, for all the shallowness of his view, he had seen me as completely as he wanted to.

* * *

The weather began to warm, a time I always dreaded. The lengthening of the days and the increase in sunlight made me feel more visible and more alone.

In the springtime, I took to wearing a denim jacket and pants with big work boots and the ski mask. The impending summer months tended to make me reckless, and I often made a last attempt at companionship before the interminable months of sun and mosquitos and humidity (which especially disagreed with my hair). I made daily trips to the coffee shop, and one day Ronnie exited as I tried to enter. He scowled, and I stepped aside, and he stepped aside, and we found ourselves mirroring each other's movements in a brief, awkward dance, until Ronnie, fed up, shouldered past me, turned, and spat at my feet. His anger deflated me, and I slumped in the doorway, listening to his footfalls recede into the distance. I waited for a moment, then walked home, skipping the café altogether.

Later that night I awoke to rustling and laughter and knew that Ronnie was back. In the morning, I didn't have the energy to clean what Ronnie had deposited near my home. Clamshell take-out trays opened and closed in the breeze, laughing at me while I sat with my hands between my knees and my back to the rocky outcropping of my home. Ronnie kept coming back, night after night, and the garbage accumulated into mounds. A doorless refrigerator, and crumpled paper towels transparent with grease, and strips of plastic and protrusions of metal covered the ground. Raccoons and rats arrived, and flies clouded the air, and I sat, unmoving, another piece of the landfill.

* * *

As daylight increased, and the sun lingered in the sky for longer, baking the refuse strewn across my yard, so too did the stench increase. One day, as I paced around, kicking aside a bent bicycle tire, I heard footsteps shuffling through the brush, and I ran to hide in my house. I crouched behind the door, waiting, and listening, and soon there was a knock.

"Sugar?"

It was Francine. I scrambled for my mask, pulling it over my face.

When I opened the door, the late afternoon sun silhouetted her form. She carried a to-go tray of coffee and a waxy paper bag, the top folded over into a little handle. She held the bag up to me.

"They're day-olds," she said, "But I thought you might want a donut. I haven't seen you in a while."

She flicked her head behind her.

"Wanna come outside?"

I nodded and we headed toward the lake. Francine explained that she had seen Ronnie spit at my feet, and then after not seeing me for a few weeks, had asked Ronnie where I lived.

"He was really worried about what you might have said about him. It was weird. Ronnie is a weird guy. He's one of those people whose story always contains a 'but.' Like, 'he's a nice guy, but.' We dated for a while, Ronnie and I. Briefly. Years ago. Anyways, I missed seeing you in the café, so I asked Ronnie what street you lived on, but I think I've been wandering all morning trying to find your house."

"You could have followed the smell."

She didn't laugh at first but waited until I winked and let her know it was fine, it was okay to laugh.

"But you missed me?"

She shrugged.

"I interact with people all day, but you would be surprised at how often customers treat me like a literal coffee maker. An appliance. Not many people ask me what I'm reading, and even then, it's because they want to tell me what *they* know about what I'm reading."

We sat down at the edge of the lake and she passed me a coffee while apologizing that it was probably cold. But I didn't mind. Francine waggled her eyebrows at me as she bit into a donut—chocolate glazed—with her hand held under her chin to catch the crumbs. Considering the state of my home, it was a kind gesture. I asked her about school. It was pleasant, listening to her voice mingle with the breeze. When she finished eating, she leaned back on her palms and pressed her face toward the sky, toward the heat of the sun, and she closed her eyes and sighed a long, lumbering breath of satisfaction. And so I sat beside her and I bathed in the sunlight on the hem of a lake in a land of garbage that was mine.

***FRANCIS WALSH** is a writer from coastal Maine. Their work appears or is forthcoming in* Brevity, *the* Los Angeles Review, *the* South Carolina Review, *the* Stonecoast Review, *and* Yemassee. *Follow them on Instagram @walshfrancis.*

A Person Who Writes

Anna Reeser

The Masters Review Vol. VII,
"Ghost Print," selected by Rebecca Makkai

At an extended family gathering this summer—my first in over a year—I was visibly pregnant, standing in the sun holding a seltzer.

A relative asked, "When are you due?" But I misheard, thinking they'd asked, *What do you do?*

"I'm a writer," I said, glowing. I went on to describe my fiction projects and my day job doing copywriting. I said "writing" multiple times in one sentence, glad to finally feel that word sit right on my tongue.

"That's…great," the relative said. "But *when* are you *due?*"

Later, I wondered if part of me had meant to mishear, had actually wanted someone to ask what I did, a question I'd dreaded until only recently.

* * *

In my twenties, I lived in Seattle and worked as a graphic designer. I had edited and designed an undergrad litmag at UC Berkeley, and when I graduated, print design was my best option for making a living. My boyfriend and I moved north, and I worked in a few harried offices (including one with "energizing" red-painted walls) before I found a stable gig at a small marketing agency where I could set my own schedule.

When new acquaintances asked what I did, I said graphic design, and I always felt a sting. I was a bad liar, and that statement felt like a partial lie. Should I mention that I also wrote short stories? That I used my flexible work schedule to carve out writing time? That I read on my bus commute? That I spent weekend afternoons revising stories and did fiction workshops at Hugo House on weeknights? That one workshop led to the monthly writing group I met in coffee shops to trade feedback, and that those meetings made me feel alive and seen? Just to get on with the flow of the conversation, I wouldn't bother.

In college, a workshop instructor had assured the class, *A writer is a person who writes.* I repeated this as a silent pep talk throughout my twenties and kept doing what I was doing. Developing characters, stretching my voice, experimenting with craft, sharing my work with trusted colleagues, and eventually submitting stories to journals. I made a convoluted spreadsheet to keep track of them. Positive rejections boosted my confidence, and I kept going. Tried to see each blue rectangle on Submittable as a possibility. But I withheld the name "writer" from myself because my path into literary fiction didn't line up with most author bios I encountered. I had built a writing life alongside an unrelated job outside of academia.

* * *

When my story "Ghost Print" was selected for *The Masters Review Volume VII* anthology, it felt like a turning point. My first print publication—and in a journal I'd admired for years. The anthology linked my name with the phrase "emerging writer." Those words felt enormous, active. At first, I wasn't sure I fit the definition.

But as I saw my name and story printed in ink—a story that had itched and hummed in a document on my screen—I realized I had given myself permission to emerge years ago. A writer is a person who writes, and I'd been writing all this time. Of course those words applied to me.

Over the next couple years, I tried out the name "writer" on myself. I kept sending out my work. I went to AWP in Portland, wearing my name on a lanyard. I told coworkers at my day job that I wrote fiction, and this led to a new role doing copywriting at the agency, a welcomed change. I packed all my sweaters for the Tin House Winter Workshop on the Oregon Coast. There, I met a cohort with whom I still exchange feedback. Each experience added to my identity as a writer, but the core of that identity was my decision to own that word, to allow its definition to apply to me.

* * *

It's been three years since my acceptance in *The Masters Review* anthology. I've had other stories published, and last year, one was selected for *The Best American Short Stories 2020*, a huge honor and surprise. I'm still emerging, but I now call this work my career. I use my spreadsheet to keep track of submissions, and I meet with my writing groups virtually to workshop stories. My husband and I moved back to California and are expecting a baby, and these new experiences are showing up in my fiction. I'm finishing a collection of stories and navigating the first stages of a novel. I'm standing around at gatherings, less awkwardly than before, ready for someone to ask what I do.

ANNA REESER *is a writer living in San Francisco. Her short fiction appears in* The Best American Short Stories 2020, The Masters Review Vol. VII *anthology,* CutBank, Fourteen Hills, *and elsewhere. She is at work on a novel and has completed a collection of short stories exploring tensions between creative obsessions, jobs, and relationships.*

Limbs

Megan Callahan

The first Arabic phrase Amir teaches me is *tisbah ala khair*. "It's a fancy way of saying goodnight," he says. We're at his Parkdale apartment. He's been living here for a month and despite being a neat freak, he can't bring himself to unpack; he says he prefers the echo of empty rooms to postmove clutter. I peel open boxes in search of glassware.

"I love the raspy fricative," I say. "It's beautiful." I'm a linguistics student, obsessed with phonetics, and every language sounds beautiful to me.

"It's wordy," he says, laughing, and rinses the tumblers in the sink. "Literally, it means *I hope you wake up to good news*. Dramatic as fuck, right?"

When I tell him that French is my mother tongue, he thinks I'm lying.

"I never lie," I say. "My dad is Francophone."

"But you don't have an accent."

"Neither do you."

He pours us arak from a tall bottle with a lime-green label while I watch from across the kitchen island, chin cupped in my palms. It's late afternoon, warm, peak summer. Amir's black curls are haloed in dusty light. We clink glasses. The arak tastes clean and botanical, like fennel seeds and cut grass. Soon I'm day-drunk, in that brief liminal space between buzzed and euphoric. We fool around on his IKEA couch, indie folk playing on loop, and I shiver with delight every time we kiss. I'm nineteen and Amir is my first real boyfriend. We've been dating a few weeks and I think I'm in love. He looks into my eyes, whispers *habibi* in my ear.

* * *

When I was little, my father taught me the names of trees: *érable rouge, bouleau blanc, noyer, sapin baumier*. Back then, the words only existed in his language. In the nature park northeast of the house, he led me down meandering pine-needle trails. I'd point to each tree and touch the crooked limbs, smell the wet earth and hanging gray moss. *Regardé*, he'd say, like he was teaching me to see. *Tu vois la coccinelle? T'as vu cette petite fleur?* I'd sprint ahead and stuff my pockets with leaves. Press them between book pages and forget them for whole seasons.

My parents split when I was twelve. They seemed relieved when they told me, as if a great weight had been lifted, so the only person who felt gutted was me. My mother kept the house, my father got the car. He bought land in Lévis and built a cottage flanking the river. In the early years, his absence was wrenching, but with time it became an ache, like a bone that healed wrong. These days, we talk less. He's beginning to sound old; on the phone his voice seems to be coming from a great distance. When he speaks, I close my eyes to better imagine him, the picture in my head unchanged, crystalline: he points to the trees. "*Ma belle dame*," he always calls me, like I'm some kind of movie star.

Sora, my oldest friend, dislikes Amir. When we met, he pretended he was still in business school. "He was ashamed of being a dropout," I argue, but Sora is unmoved. My mother, a staunch Catholic who equates the Middle East with women's oppression, berates me with questions. "Is he controlling?" she asks. "Does he let you go out?" When we visit, she's polite. Her smiles are cool and suspicious. So, when my father asks about Amir, I tell him only the most endearing anecdotes: the time he surprised me after class with daffodils; how he braved a blizzard to soothe my ice cream craving. It's been almost a year and I know he's the one. I'm secretly planning the trajectory of our future: We'll go to Beirut and I'll charm his parents. Amir will propose on a beach, under the stars. At our late-autumn wedding, our mothers will bond over tea and rice pudding. Our fathers will be like long-lost brothers. We'll be a new family: one tree branching out into pairs of smaller limbs.

That evening, I tell Amir I want to take an Arabic elective.

"Why?" He's leaning over a skillet, caramelizing onions for *mujadara*, and the tangy, sweet smell permeates the room. I know it will linger in my sweater for weeks.

"It's your mother tongue," I say.

"But we speak English together." He looks at me, bemused. "And they only teach Classical Arabic, which is like…Old English. It would take you years to get good enough to speak my dialect."

Months later, I mention the class again. We're moving in together. Our lives are becoming more entwined. But again, he dissuades me. His tone is gentle but firm, like he's doing me a favor. My rational brain accepts his arguments. But secretly, in my heart, I believe he's trying to tell me something. His reassuring words ring like coded messages: *I'm just having fun,* or *I'm not sure about us.* Or, worst of all: *I lied when I said I loved you.*

* * *

Every day, my homesickness grows. I miss Montréal, my family, my friends. "Really?" Amir asks, with genuine confusion. He is enamored with Toronto, the pulsing energy and skyscrapers. His favorite bars have dress codes and shiny leather seats. They serve creatively named cocktails that neither of us can afford. "One day, we'll be regulars," he prophesizes, slapping cash on the polished table like it's nothing. I nod and smile; when he gets like this, swept up in some pretend vision of our life, that's all I can do. In our sardine-can apartment, the walls are thin. I can hear our neighbors when they fight, when they have sex in the shower. On weekends, the sirens and street noise keep me awake. I go out on the balcony and watch the crowds below trickle in and out of bars, my body heavy from sleeplessness.

One morning in March, I drag my suitcase from the closet.

"I'm going home for spring break," I announce.

The sky outside is pigeon-gray, the streets below puddled with slush. Amir is sitting on the unmade bed, laptop on his knees. "This is home," he says, without looking up.

I cross my arms. "My mom's home," I say, bristling at his irritation. Our arguments have a well-rehearsed choreography: he leads, I follow. "You don't have to come."

"Obviously I'll come," he counters, like I've insulted him. "It's just hard, not understanding half of what people say." I interpret this to mean, *I will never learn French. I don't love you enough to learn.*

"Anyways," he says. "Didn't we just see her?"

Amir relishes being thousands of miles away from his family. He Skypes with them sporadically, at odd hours, and weaves stories about his make-believe degree. Neither of his parents suspect. They still transfer him tuition money, believing he's going to be an entrepreneur or an accountant. They're saving up to invest in his start-up. When I coax Amir to come clean, he gives me the same incredulous look. "There's so much pressure. Expectations. They'd never understand." My mental image of his parents is a messy collage of facts and photographs: his father is taciturn and works in textiles; his mother cuts hair and goes to mosque every Friday. I don't know what Amir tells them about me.

What they don't know is that Amir wants to be an actor. When he's on stage, I see a different side of him. He screams, rages, cries real tears. I have never seen him cry in real life. As soon as the lights dim, he locks up those colorful emotions with the props and costumes.

Last summer he was cast as Mercutio in a modern retelling of *Romeo and Juliet*, and the reviews were good. Amir quit his dishwasher job. "This is it," he'd predicted, with rock-solid certainty. But with winter came a lull: no plays, no calls. He hasn't been to an audition in over a month. These days his only gig is at the Baycrest Hospital as a standardized patient, where he pretends to faint or have a seizure while terrified, baby-faced residents attempt to make a diagnosis.

Eventually, I relent. We agree to make the drive next month, when it's warmer. I shove my bag into the closet and ignore the twinge in my gut. More than anything, I miss speaking French. Whenever I call my father, there are gaps where words should be. I don't want to admit it, but I'm losing the language.

* * *

Amir breaks up with me on a Sunday. He makes us Lebanese breakfast: warm *foul* and olive oil, fresh pita from the dep on the corner. Snow drifts past the window, the thin chalky kind that signals arctic cold. We sit at the kitchen island in our thickest socks, eating with our hands in sleepy silence. I'm distracted, my thoughts on school. I have an exam on Monday—*covert Wh-movement*. Class notes scroll through my mind and I see the syntax trees, each phrase branching out into pairs of smaller limbs. Amir is jittery. He doesn't finish his food. As I wipe my plate clean, he stands abruptly, like he's been waiting for this precise moment.

"I want to break up," he declares. Eyes downcast, voice measured. Something twists violently in my gut. We've been together for just over two years.

Amir tells me he's been thinking about it for a while. "About a month," he states, without a trace of guilt or shame. I'm mute. He's been playacting for weeks and I didn't notice. My stomach tightens and cramps. I lurch from my chair, rush to the bathroom, and throw up in the sink. For a moment I stare at the undigested bean sludge. Amir brings me a glass of water but can't meet my gaze. "Why?" I manage, but he won't give me a reason.

I leave the apartment in a haze, carrying nothing, and walk the four blocks to Sora's doorstep. She makes me soup and lets me sob into her shoulder. "Maybe it's for the best," she says tentatively. "You can date around. Have fun." Everything she says makes me want to scream.

Three days pass. I bomb my exam, skip every other class. Speaking is painful; eating requires great effort. I'm dying, I think. I might as well be dead.

On Wednesday night, Amir shows up at Sora's door.

Stunned, I let him in. Hovering in the doorway, he looks small. Feet shuffling, face flushed from the cold. He's obviously been crying, and this makes me angry—he still has never cried in front of me.

"Is Sora here?" he asks.

"She's out."

"She hates me even more now, huh?"

I raise my eyebrows. Wait for him to speak.

"I made a mistake," he says. His words are timid. "I don't know why I did it."

The silence spreads out. I hear the rumble of Sora's dryer, the muddled voices of her neighbors. Amir stares at his hands, looking pitiful in the lamp light. For a moment I'm able to hold on to my anger, to brandish it forward like an invisible shield. But as soon as he looks up, I know that I've lost. My outrage swells, crests, and dissipates.

We have sex on the couch and it feels new, thrilling. Every kiss is profound, every touch suffused with meaning. *Habibi*, Amir says, and I smile. I drink it in. He falls asleep on my chest, slender arm resting on the curve of my belly, and for a while I listen to the steady flow of his breaths and feel weightless.

* * *

My father dies the summer I turn twenty-three. Heart attack. Sudden. A neighbor spots him through the slats of their shared fence, lying stiff in the garden beneath the flowering pink azaleas. I cry when my mother tells me, but it's a distant kind of sadness. I'd already been losing him, day by day, and this was simply the last inevitable step.

Amir and I drive to Montréal for the burial. A brief service is held in a white-stone chapel encircled by hydrangeas. Uncles and aunts I haven't seen in years grasp my hand, reminisce about my childhood. "*Quelle tragédie*," they lament, and I nod, feeling numb. Amir clings to my arm, lost in a sea of French. We sit with my relatives in the front pew, knee to knee, and I wonder if being included in the family section makes Amir uncomfortable. He plays with his tie, taps his shoe against the tiles.

After the service we pack into the cars and follow the hearse through the landscaped cemetery. It's a humid day. Cerulean sky with puffs of clouds. Late afternoon, peak summer, but there won't be drinks until later. I watch the casket being lowered into the ground, holding my mother's hand. The moment is disappointing. People die sometimes, I realize, and the world stays the same. Afterward I cry in the back of the car while Amir passes me tissues, face turned to the window.

At my mother's suburban house, we eat condolence casserole and drink cheap Merlot. My mother barely speaks, her puffy eyes looking inward at some private, distant memory. I gather the dishes as she slips off to bed, swaying on her feet. Afterward I sit on the back porch and light a cigarette. Amir is beside me, arm slung around my bare shoulders. It's strange, to be so close to him and yet feel so far away. His phone buzzes and he shows me the caller ID, asking with his eyes—*Can I take this?* I nod and force a smile. He stands and walks the length of the porch, talking with his mother. I hear my name in the flow of Arabic and focus my mind, trying to pick out the words.

Amir still doesn't know that I signed up for that elective. The secret is thrilling. Soon I'll be able to piece together whole phrases. A language can be a bridge; it can change the way you see things. I blow smoke into the darkness and allow myself to imagine it: One day, I'll surprise Amir with flawless Arabic. I'll turn to him in bed and say *tisbah ala khair*, uttering that pharyngeal fricative like I was born to it. *Habibi*, I'll say, and he'll know that he's home.

Behind my mother's property is a small, green park. I recognize the trees but can't remember their French names. How do you say white oak? How do you say balsam fir? My mind comes up empty, like the words have been misplaced or maybe lost forever. Every day, I lose another. I grope for these words and feel the spaces they've left behind. I grieve for them as if they were once alive. As if they were once part of my own body, limbs I didn't even know I had.

MEGAN CALLAHAN is a writer, book reviewer, and French-to-English translator. Her work has appeared in literary magazines like Nashville Review, Room, *and* PRISM international, *and in the* 2021 Best Canadian Stories *anthology. She lives and works in Tiohtià:ke/Montréal.*

Resurrection

Hilary Dean

When we met Gianni in Miss Thompson's grade-eight class, he had failed it twice already and didn't even care.

"Rocky Balboa flunked school too," he said. "I'm just like him. An Italian stallion."

He was fifteen. We turned thirteen one by one that year and he continued to tower over us. We had no chance of catching up. Gianni had real muscles and he shaved. When we learned about *The Voyage of Puberty* in health class, he looked like the drawing on the pamphlet's last page.

"I know all this already," he said. "I took that freakin' voyage."

He knew everything already, the whole curriculum. He'd even memorized Miss Thompson's routines and little jokes about integers and *Treasure Island* and Louis Riel.

"He was a *Riel* hero, ha ha," Gianni would lip-sync along with her while he peeled the glue off his desk. He liked to dab little white glue blobs and then watch them dry into clear discs, which he'd then peel off and add to the pile inside his desk. He had like a million glue blobs. I sat beside him, so I appreciated the growing collection firsthand. It seemed satisfying and somehow useful, in a way that my desk full of exploding fire cloud drawings was not.

"Gianni."

Miss Thompson would say his name with a soft, practiced patience. She'd stare at him until he looked up from his glue to meet her gaze. Her eyes were heavily lined with a shimmery green color that made her look like a lizard wearing the face mask of a nice lady.

"If you know the answer, Gianni, then why don't you raise your hand?"

He would just shrug. He never raised his hand.

He kept failing. He failed hard and he failed on purpose. He didn't hand in any homework assignments. He would leave tests blank, or draw skulls on them, with sometimes a speech bubble coming out of the skull's mouth that said, *I! DON'T! CARE!*

He'd play sports at recess, but in gym class he'd just sit on the floor, re-safety-pinning the cuffs of his acid-washed jeans. He wouldn't try. He wouldn't even *try*.

I didn't get what his deal was because I tried so hard. I studied every night, memorizing names and dates. I used a ruler to make straight lines. I listened to Miss Thompson and Madame LeGuin and Father Sam. I behaved how they said to and even tried to think how they said to because God was fully psychic and could read my mind at any time. He could just drop in there whenever He wanted to and eavesdrop on me, so I tried to think nicely. On class trips to Confession, I was somber and penitent because I truly wanted to have a pure soul. I knew for sure I had to avoid hell, but I also couldn't risk ending up in purgatory for all of eternity, babysitting the crying unbaptized limbo babies forever so I tried very hard to be good. I couldn't understand not trying at all.

"Adrian?"

"Here!" I said.

"Gianni?"

"..."

"Gianni."

"I changed my name, Miss. To Stu. Stu Gots."

"Just say *Here*, Gianni. Or *Present*."

"Here." He rolled his eyes. "I have a present for you," he whispered. "Stugots."

I laughed at that. I couldn't help it.

"Hey, you get that, Aidge? You know what that means, white girl? Mangia-cake?"

"Yeah, duh, Gio," I whispered. "You're white too, by the way. Don't act like you're not."

"Nuh-uh."

Ever since we learned about racism, it was the worst, most uncool thing to be white. Richmond Hill was mostly Chinese, South Asian, and Black, and then out of the ten white kids in class, the Italian half decided they weren't white anymore after we found out about slavery. They started calling the rest of us white and demanding that we apologize for what our ancestors had done. We swore that we never even *knew* them, we were just hearing about this whole thing *now* and we felt horrible about it. That might have blown over, but then we got to World War Two and Miss Thompson made the five of us who had blue eyes stand at the front of the room. She said we would have been the only ones to survive the Holocaust and everyone booed us.

"Anyways," I told Gianni, "I'm only three-quarters mangia-cake."

"Naw, you're a cake. You have yellow hair. Cake hair."

"My hair is dark blonde. It is *ash* blonde. And anyway, guess what? Everyone eats cake. At every Italian party I've ever been to, there is a *ton* of cake. Italians eat cake all the time, especially that kind with the rum in it and the almond slices, and the black forest with the cherries. I bet you eat cake too, Gianni. I bet you *love* it."

He raised his eyebrows, impressed. "That's true, Aidge," he said. "I do love cake. My mom used to make the best cakes, oh man. I used to be the biggest mangia-cake of all."

* * *

When Miss Thompson held auditions for the school play, she said everyone had to try out. "It is *man*datory," she said. "Man-da-tor-*y*."

Brent the Bus-Barfer went first. He recited his favorite song like it was Shakespeare.

"Kiss her," he said with a dramatic fake British accent. "Miss her... Love her. That girl is poison." He shook his head sadly.

Fiona recited her public speaking assignment, even though I'd warned her not to because no one was done making fun of it yet.

"I won third place at *Regionals*," she hissed at me, all offended.

"Step! Hop, hop," she recited. "Step! Hop, hop. Step! Hop, hop. This is the sound of Terry Fox running his way across Canada on one prosthetic leg!"

"Miss?" Jen B. said. "I know I sang already? But should I do *my* speech again too?"

"Oh no," Miss Thompson said quickly. "No, thank you, that's not necessary at all, Jennifer. You sang beautifully."

"You can say it to us again at recess," I whispered.

The rest of the girls nodded. We never got tired of Jen B.'s speech about her older sister being murdered in America and the killer never being found even to this day. At every séance we kept getting more clues and one day our powers would be strong enough to solve the case and put the killer in jail.

"It's your turn, Gianni," Miss Thompson said, gesturing to the front of the room.

He walked up slowly and just stood there. "I don't got nothing," he said.

"Why don't you do what Brent did?" Miss Thompson said. "Say the words to a song in a loud, clear voice."

"Naw," Gianni said. "I'll just do my mom's soap, I guess. It's easy." He cleared his throat.

"*Run away with me!*" he yelled passionately. "*We were meant to be together. I know you feel the same way.*"

"*I can't!*" he cried in a lady voice, turning to face the other direction. "*I'm in love with someone else!*"

"*Who is it?*" he yelled in the man voice again. "*Tell me who it is, damn it. Tell me his damn name, damn it.*"

"*It's- It's- It's- It's Bradley,*" Gianni sobbed like a lady.

"Then this other guy comes in," he said. "It's a cop, I'm the cop now. *I have some terrible, shocking news. This news that I have right now is going to shock you so much. Bradley is dead. And it's shocking.*"

"*Oh my god, no! Not my Bradley, oh my god…* And this is my mom, crying on the couch, *Oh no, that's terrible. Bradley was my favorite character, oh no.* And then my dad comes in, *Goddamn it, Sabrina, what are you crying about now? All you do is sit on the couch and cry all day, you never even leave the house anymore. That same nightgown for a week, you're disgusting. I swear to god, as soon as the kid's in high school I'm gonna—*"

"Thank you, Gianni," Miss Thompson said. "That's— I'm going to stop you there, that was great. Really good job. I think that someone has found their true calling. Don't you think, class? Oh, Fiona, would you hand me my clipboard there?"

"Sure," Fiona said, going to grab it.

"Step hop hop!" Yolanda yelled.

"Shut up!" Fiona said, as everyone cracked up laughing. "Oh my gosh, I hate you guys! I wish Terry Fox was still alive instead of all of you!"

So that's how Gianni got the lead in the school play. He got to play Jesus, but I got the best part of all: Mary Magdalene. All the other girls were so jealous because there were only three female roles in the whole play: Mother Mary, Mary Magdalene, and Cousin Martha who had only one line.

My costume was a flouncy gypsy dress and tons of makeup. The other girls had to play old men and wear gross, fake, itchy beards glued onto them with spirit gum.

"Will you please, please trade with me?" Melissa said, who was Caiaphas the High Priest.

"Sure," I said. "Psych. *No dice.*"

"Could you trade with *me*?" Erica asked. "They're making me play a leper, it's not fair. I know it's because of my scar." She pouted and made sad eyes at me.

"Sorry," I said. "Miss Thompson said that I'm not allowed to trade."

That was a lie, and being sorry about it was also a lie, but I'd just tell Father Sam at next Confession and then I'd be pure again like it never even happened.

I was in a lot of scenes but Gianni was in every single one. We were performing almost the entire New Testament, including a dance number at the wedding where water gets turned into wine. It was mostly just a lot of hopping but we still practiced a lot.

"This is a very ambitious production," Miss Thompson said. "We're going to begin with Jesus meeting John the Baptist—that's you, Yolanda—and we'll end with the Resurrection."

"I have a question," Gianni said. "Who is Rez? And why does he got an erection?"

"Enough," Miss Thompson said. "Stop laughing, everyone. That is highly inappropriate. Gianni, come on. You were doing so well. No more jokes. Let's focus on what's important."

"Jokes are important, Miss."

Miss Thompson sighed. "I'm going to invite Father Sam to come down from the high school and speak to us about Jesus. We can ask him questions and learn from him and I think that will help some of us…better embody…our roles."

Any time Father Sam was coming to our class it was like a celebrity was visiting. We usually only saw him from far away at the altar at church, so to see him up close and get special attention was like an honor. We'd all pretend we were too cool to care that he was coming but then we'd scramble for spots on the floor up close to him to get pats on the head from his magic God hands.

"So, where should we start?" Father Sam said. "What would you like to know about Jesus?"

"Gianni?" Miss Thompson prompted.

"Is he real?" Gianni said.

"Jesus?" Father Sam asked. "Is Jesus real? Of course he's real."

"No, but, like, is it that thing where everyone says he's real but then you find out later he isn't, like Santa Claus and the Easter Bunny and the Tooth Fairy?"

"No," Father Sam said. "He's definitely real. He was a real, living man, who was the son of God. And He died for us. He died for our sins. And He's alive today, living in our hearts."

"Are aliens real?"

"No."

"Is the Sasquatch real?"

"Gianni," Father Sam said, "playing Jesus Christ is a great responsibility and it's going to take a lot of maturity. But I know you can handle it. I have faith in you, and so does Miss Thompson. You are going to be a wonderful Jesus."

And he was. He was an incredible Jesus. He stopped shaving and grew out his own beard and he memorized all his lines. He even adopted a soft, Jesus-y voice that he'd use during recess to break up fights.

He was very nice to me dressed as Jesus. He told me that he'd make sure his feet were clean so that when I had to anoint them with oil I wouldn't be grossed out. And when everyone gathered around to stone me for being a prostitute, Gianni picked me up from the floor so kindly and gently that I honestly felt like I loved him, the way I loved the real Jesus.

"Bud, you are such a good actor," I told him.

"Ya bud, I know," he said. "I'm acting like such a good actor."

"Just watch," Krish said. We sometimes walked home from school together and we always argued the whole way. "Gianni's going to be bad."

"He is not."

"Why do you always want to take the long way, Adrian?"

"It's better. More graffiti, plus the creek."

"What's so big about the creek?"

Nothing, I just had to avoid this one boy's house. This one boy who beat me up one time when a bunch of us were playing in my backyard at a barbecue. I'd gone inside crying and told my mom what had happened and then she pulled me into the bathroom and told me that the boy was messed up inside his mind and had serious problems because his father raped his mother in high school and she got pregnant and they decided to get married and pretend that it wasn't really a rape but everyone in the neighborhood knew that their son was a rape baby and their whole marriage was a lie. So I had to pretend that I didn't know either and clean myself up and eat dinner with everyone and act like everything was fine, because that's what grown-ups did. So then I sat there holding an ice pack over my face and we all ate hamburgers: me, my family, the rape-baby kid who didn't even get in trouble for punching me over and over, and his mom who got raped by his dad who was a rapist sitting across from me smiling but never tell anyone.

"Nothing."

"I bet you anything Gio is going to go balls-out crazy in the temple scene. Instead of just knocking over a few merchants' pillars, he is going to *trash* the place."

"I don't think so," I said. We'd reached my house and were standing at the end of my driveway. Without looking at Krish, I casually smelled him as hard as I could, hoping he wouldn't notice. He wore Cool Water cologne, so he always smelled like a fun dance party with potato chips on pizza and Seven-Minutes-in-Heaven-No-Tongues.

"Trust me," he said. "He's going to mess it up. He's like his mom. You know how his mom is..." He pointed to his head and did slow circles.

"That's not true. I would have heard about it."

"Yeah, like you know everything. They put her in a straightjacket and locked her up. They only let her out after they removed *five* pieces of her *brain*. And when they *saw* the pieces, they were *black*. And then a crucifix fell off the *wall*. Because her brain was possessed by *Satan*."

"Whatever," I said, checking my unicorn watch. There were important things I had to take care of right after school so I needed to get inside. But I also felt like I should defend Gianni. He had come to my defense so many times, even though it was really Mary Magdalene's defense.

"That's not even science, first," I said. "Plus there's no crosses in operating rooms, I'm not stupid. You're just being gross because you're jealous that you didn't get to be Jesus. Gianni is going to be perfect. He's *totally* changed. He's even handing in homework and doing gym. I bet after this, he's going to go to Hollywood and everyone will ask him for his autograph and you will be *so, so* even *more* jealous."

"*Not*. Later, Prostitute Mary."

"*Bye*, Pharisee Number Five."

I walked through the kitchen, past Travis and Chris who were whipping Cocoa Pebbles at each other's faces. In the TV room, I reached for my VHS of *La Bamba* but it wasn't there.

"Looking for *this*?" Travis appeared in the doorway, waving the tape at me.

"Give it," I said.

"Why? You already watched it yesterday. You watch it every day."

"Give it to me *now* or I'll tell Mom you opened a whole new cereal before the old one was finished."

"Fine. I mean, *oops*." He dropped the tape on the floor.

"Fuck you, Fuck-Ass!" Fuck. Another thing I had to confess. Two things. Fuck. Three things.

Then Chris's fat little angel face peered around the door. He smiled at me.

"You said a very bad word, Adrian Green," he whispered.

"I'm sorry," I whispered back. "But what I am doing is very, very important."

"Okay," he sang as he ran down the hall. A few seconds later the blast from his tape player filled the house.

Hello, Christopher, how do you do? I'm gonna sing some songs for you! Some fast songs, some slow songs, some funny songs too! And Christopher, all the songs are all about you! We're gonna sing about Christopher! We're gonna sing about Christopher! We're gonna sing about Christopher! 'Cause he's a special boy..."

I closed the door, put the tape in the VCR and rewound the video to the beginning. I watched *La Bamba* until Buddy Holly, Ritchie Valens, The Big Bopper, and the pilot were about to get on the plane. Then, before they could, I stopped the tape and saved all their lives. Then I went upstairs to my room, did my homework, added the new sins to my diary, wrote some nice-girl stuff in my decoy diary for my mom to spy on, ran through my Mary lines, then practiced looking holy and pitiful in front of the mirror for half an hour.

Dinner was pot roast. I could eat it until I got a fatty bit but then once I did, the whole thing was over. No more chances.

"Madame LeGuin is a total B-word," Travis said.

"I do everything. You do nothing."

"She doesn't even know French good," I said. "Like, it's all just like—"

"I work all day. What do you think I do all day, Cindy?"

"—It's all just *vocabulaire*? Like we're not even learning French, just random words. Like, *biblioteche. Bonhomme. Chevalle.*"

"Christopher, let the fun begin! It's bath time, Christopher, dive in!"

"You think school isn't work?"

"Ooh, point goes to Mom there. I know, it's like if we ever go to France or Quebec, we'll just point at things and say their names."

I laughed and pretended to point. "*L'ananas!*"

"I'm working as hard as I can. I'm trying to educate myself."

"I know. Who do you think is paying for your education?"

"At least she likes you though. Every teacher automatically hates me because they have you first and then two years later they get me. And they're like, Why aren't you like your sister? Why aren't you like Adri—"

"I'm exhausted. But I still have to come home and cook and clean. I have to do everything all by myself."

"You think I'm not exhausted? You think after the day I had, I need to sit here and listen to this?"

"Teachers are so easy though, Travis. You just do what they say and then they're happy and that's it."

"Rub-a-dub-a-dub-ah! In the bath!"

* * *

Krish was wrong in his prediction. Gianni blew our minds in the final dress rehearsal.

"He was so good, Aidge," Yolanda said, as we walked to her house. "Shit. Fuck."

She pointed to the white van behind us and we took off but she was still wearing her sandals from the play and couldn't run good.

"Just kick them off, Yolie," I said. She slipped one off and then the other, holding onto my shoulder for balance.

"Girls!" the van guy yelled. "Come here, I just want to show you something."

We cut across her neighbor's lawn, through their backyard, and walked the rest of the way along the ravine.

Yolanda told me that when she baptized Gio in the blue cardboard river, he had actual tears in his actual eyes.

"He said that when he wants to get tears, he just thinks of the *Fresh Prince* episode where Will gave Carlton drugs by accident."

We were both very moved by this. Carlton had almost died.

* * *

I tried to think of that same episode when I watched Gianni being crucified but it didn't work for me. I couldn't cry.

"Think of the Challenger exploding," said Gianni. "You were there on the beach, right? In Florida? Your mom told my mom she felt bad for taking you."

"Yeah, but I don't remember. It was in grade one."

"Just cover your face with your hands then and shake your shoulders a bit. Sometimes crying people rock back and forth too, you could do that."

"Thank you, Jesus."

"You're welcome, my child."

I convinced everyone to let Gianni come to the next séance because I knew he had the for-real actual Spirit within him now and could help us get closer to the Next Realm. But I forgot to tell him that it was a séance and he freaked out when he got there.

"Yo, what the hell?" he said, looking at all the candles. "This is some spooky shit, yo."

"Don't worry," Melissa said. "We'll be your guides." She brought out her red and yellow plastic Speak & Spell toy. We used it because its batteries were close to wearing out, so the robot voice had become all warbled and satanic. She typed into the Speak & Spell and placed it on the floor.

Bloooooood. Saaaaaaaaay iiiiiiiit. Eviiiiiiiiiillllllll. Saaaaaaaaay iiiiiiiit.

"What the hell is that?" Gianni said. Then he saw the ouija board and jumped back.

"I'm not touching that thing, oh my god. You guys don't know? Yo, yo, open the light. Listen to me. Anything could come through there, okay? Not just nice spirits, *you* don't know. You use that thing and *demons* could come through, I'm telling you. Evil shit is nothing to joke about, it can possess you through those boards. My mom said even *The Devil* came through this one time to this girl she knew and she was *fucked*, man. She was haunted for*ever*."

"Okay, okay," Yolanda said, rolling her eyes.

"Let's do levitation," Jen B. said. "I'm the priest."

"Yes!" Melissa said. "It's my turn to be dead." We explained everything to Gianni and showed him the hand positions. Melissa lay on the floor with her eyes closed and her arms crossed over her chest. Jen B. turned the lights off again and knelt behind Melissa, cradling her head.

"Dearly Beloved, we are gathered here today to levitate the soul of our dear friend Melissa," Jen B. intoned. "She was a wonderful person and we will miss her so very much. Melissa would always ask me what was wrong when I felt sad."

"Every time Melissa had a birthday party," I said, "she invited the whole class, even people who sucked, just so that no one would get hurt feelings."

"When Melissa's sister would pull her hair and beat her up, Melissa would just take it. She never fought back. She was a pacifist," Fiona said.

"Melissa always shared all her candy and snacks at recess, and she'd never just drop two or three Nerds in your hand, she'd open the hole all the way up and really shake it hard so you'd get a lot, and no one else ever did that," Erica said.

"When the bee stung me at the Observatory, Melissa did the EpiPen on my thigh and saved my life," Natalie said.

"When Melissa had bingo, she traded her card with me so that I could yell bingo and get bingo," Yolanda said.

"Melissa was very nice and very pretty," Gianni said.

"Ashes to ashes," Jen B. said. "Dust to dust. Light as a feather."

"Light as a feather, light as a feather, light as a feather," we chanted. "Stiff as a board, stiff as a board, stiff as a board."

"We will now raise her soul."

We lifted Melissa as high as we could, and because Gianni was there, we could hold her all the way above our heads. She was supposed to stay silent, but she laughed with excitement.

"I'm flying!" she said.

Gianni whispered in the dark. "You guys are psychos, eh?"

* * *

The night of the big performance, Miss Thompson told me and Gianni that she'd reserved seats for our parents in the front row.

"Because you two have the biggest parts," she said. "Adrian, your dad is so funny. When I asked if he was coming to the play, he said, *She's in a play?* Ha ha. As if you wouldn't tell your parents about a play we've been rehearsing for months."

"Ha ha," I said.

"But my mom can't come," Gianni said. "She's sick."

"Well, she must be feeling better because I called her and she's on her way. She's very proud of you, Gianni. We all are. I told her there's no doubt in my mind that you're going to get an A+ in drama. And with the work you've been doing in your other subjects, you're guaranteed to graduate this year. I'd love to write you a letter of recommendation to Unionville High School. I think you'd be perfect for their theater program."

"Gianni," I said, "that's awesome. You'll totally get in."

"She's on her way?"

"I called and invited her myself," Miss Thompson said. "I wanted to make sure she knew how important tonight was."

That night, we performed better than we ever had. The audience was entranced by us, like the magic of The Holy Bible had cast a spell on them. The stage was lined with fake prop candles and our costumes glowed in the light. No one forgot a line or made a single mistake. No one smirked at each other or rubbed their beards off.

Saying my lines, I felt the Holy Spirit glowing within me for real and I think everyone did. Something in the atmosphere, something still and graceful came over us, and we weren't thirteen-year-old kids anymore. We were the astounded witnesses of a profound and tragic story. We believed in it and it became real.

As I mimed washing Gianni's feet, he whispered to me:
"Mangia-cake."
I looked up at him. He smiled.
"You're doing great," he said. "I'm very proud of you."

He turned water into wine and raised Lazarus from the dead. He healed the sick and he smashed up the temple. He was betrayed by Judas and condemned to death by Pontius Pilate.

Then he was up on the cross. Jen B. and Natalie were pretending to whip him with pieces of string attached to painted pop cans.

"We have no king but Caesar!" Natalie yelled.

I knelt at the foot of the cross and pretended to cry. As Gianni flinched and cried out in pain, I looked up and saw Miss Thompson standing at the side of the stage. She had her hands pressed over her heart. Thin rivers of green makeup ran down her face. She was crying for real.

At the end of that scene, everything went dark. When the lights came on, Mother Mary and John were frantic. They told me that the stone of the tomb had been rolled away and that Jesus was gone. His body wasn't there. They were freaking out and they ran away to look for help.

I was alone. Suddenly there were footsteps. I looked up and there was Jesus, standing before me.

"You're alive!" I yelled. "But you were dead, master! I saw you die!"

"No," Jesus said. He walked to the middle of the stage and opened his arms to the audience. "That was my identical twin brother on that cross. My brother Jesus who looks exactly like me. I planned this whole thing. I'm Jesus's evil twin, Bradley! I'm alive and I've come back to you, Sabrina! Bradley's alive!"

Miss Thompson did nothing. She just stood there with her eyes closed, as if she had fallen asleep standing up. The apostles in the wings stood frozen, gaping at Gianni. The auditorium went silent. Then out of the darkness came a loud and beautiful laugh from the woman sitting front row center.

HILARY DEAN *is currently seeking representation for her novel,* Dolly Zoom, *of which "Resurrection" is the first chapter. Other excerpts have won CBC's Canada Writes award in 2012, EVENT Magazine's Non-Fiction contest twice, been named as a Notable Essay in* Best American Essays 2015, *received the 2016 Lascaux Prize in Fiction, appeared in* This Magazine, Matrix, The HG Wells Anthology, Bath Flash Fiction, *and shortlisted for the Journey and Commonwealth Prizes. Dean's documentary film,* So You're Going Crazy. . . *aired on Canadian television for a decade and continues to be utilized in healthcare curricula and peer support networks worldwide. You can find more of her work at www.hilarydean.ca*